No escape!

I took three deep breaths, loosened up the muscles in my soldiers, and prepared my mental energies for an emergency procedure we call Doggie Battering Ram. We very seldom use it and very seldom need it. Now . . . we need it.

And so it was that, after preparing myself mentally and physically for this dangerous escape procedure, I coiled my legs under me, hurled myself like a cannonball at the window, and . . .

BONK!

Holy smokes, I was trapped inside a runaway pickup!

The Case of the
Haystack Kitties

The Case of the
Haystack Kitties

John R. Erickson

Illustrations by Gerald L. Holmes

Puffin Books

PUFFIN BOOKS
Published by the Penguin Group
Penguin Putnam Books for Young Readers,
345 Hudson Street, New York, New York 10014, U.S.A.
Penguin Books Ltd,
27 Wrights Lane, London W8 5TZ, England
Penguin Books Australia Ltd,
Ringwood, Victoria, Australia
Penguin Books Canada Ltd,
10 Alcorn Avenue, Toronto, Ontario, Canada M4V 3B2
Penguin Books (N.Z.) Ltd,
182-190 Wairau Road, Auckland 10, New Zealand

Penguin Books Ltd, Registered Offices:
Harmondsworth, Middlesex, England

First published in the United States of America
by Maverick Books, Gulf Publishing Company, 1998
Published by Puffin Books, a member of
Penguin Putnam Books for Young Readers, 1999

11 13 15 17 19 20 18 16 14 12

ISBN 978-0-14-130406-9

Hank the Cowdog® is a registered trademark of John R. Erickson.

Printed in the United States of America

For two new Hank fans:
Kale Todd Erickson and David Rinker

CONTENTS

I Catch Drover
Doing Ridiculous
Things

It's me again, Hank the Cowdog. The day began just as many other days had started. I barked up the sun exactly at daylight, barked at a mockingbird that was making a nuisance of himself in one of those elm trees near the gas tanks, and did a routine patrol of the corrals.

Little did I know or suspect that before the day was done, I would be trapped in a runaway pickup or that I would discover a nest of trespassing stray cats in the haystack. Or that I would do battle with a raging bull.

Pretty busy day, huh? But I didn't know any of that, and you're not supposed to know it

1

either, so just forget that I mentioned it.

In every way, it appeared to be just another day on the ranch, a normal day in other words, in the late spring or early summer. The first of May, I guess it was. Yes, because Sally May had planted her garden, and the chinaberry trees were beginning to bloom, and the cottonwoods along the creek had begun putting out cotton.

Have we discussed cottonwoods and cotton? Maybe not. Cottonwood trees are called cottonwood trees for three reasons. Number One, they are trees. Number Two, their trunks contain wood. And Number Three, the leafy portion of the tree produces little seeds that resemble puffs of cotton, and in the springtime the air is filled with them.

Hencely, if you put those three elements together—tree, wood, and cotton—you come up with the name of the tree. No, wait a minute. If you put them together, you'd come up with . . . hang on just a second whilst I do some figuring . . . you'd come up with "treewood cotton," which is *not* the name of the tree. It's not the name of anything. It's gibberish.

So what we have to do is take those same three elements—tree, wood, and cotton—and *reverse the order,* see, and that gives us the correct answer, which is "cottonwood tree."

Pretty slick, huh? You bet it is. How many dogs can tell you everything about trees? Not many. Very few. Most of your ordinary ranch mutts have only one use for a tree and couldn't care less about where the name comes from.

You might be wondering what this discussion of cottonwood trees has to do with the mysteries that were about to unfold on that particular day. Well . . . not much, actually, except that when I returned to my office around eight o'clock that morning, I caught Drover in the act of . . . you won't believe this. Even I found it hard to believe.

I mean, I've served on this ranch with Drover for . . . how many years? A lot. We've shared the same bedroom-office under the gas tanks, worked many cases together, solved many mysteries, shared the same bowl of Co-op dog food, and you'd think that after all that, I would have seen every dumb stunt that Drover could come up with.

Nope. On that particular morning, I caught the little mutt . . . *chasing puffs of cottonwood cotton.* That was a new one. I'd watched him chase butter-flies, grasshoppers, frogs, and crickets. I'd seen him snap at snowflakes and cinders from burning garbage. But I had never supposed that I would . . . so forth, but I did.

I sat down on my gunnysack bed and watched.

He was so wrapped up in his little adventure, he didn't even notice me.

Here came a puff of cotton floating through the air. Drover spotted it and crouched down.

He watched it coming. His ears were up, and his eyes were locked on the target. When it passed overhead, he sprang into the air and snapped at it. He missed, of course, and hurled himself at it again and snapped again, and landed on his back in the dirt.

I guess he caught it the second time. Anyway, it disappeared.

Well, that was enough. I rose from my gunnysack and marched over to him. He was still lying on the ground, huffing and puffing, and looking pretty proud of himself.

"Oh, hi Hank. Did you see what I just did?"

"Yes, I saw it, the whole thing."

"Pretty good, huh? I snapped it right out of the air, and I got it on the first shot."

"You got it on the second shot."

"Oh. Maybe that was it. I almost got it on the first shot, and then I sure 'nuff got it on the second."

I took a deep breath and looked around to see if we were alone. What I had to say was going to be embarrassing, and I didn't want anyone outside of the Security Division to hear it.

"Drover, we need to have a little talk."

4

"We do?"

"Yes, we do. It has come to my attention that you often engage in behavior that is . . . how shall I put this?"

"Well, I don't know. Heroic?"

"No."

"Courageous and bold?"

"No."

"Outstanding? Athletic?"

"I'll supply the words, Drover. You just listen."

"Well, you asked."

"I'm sorry I asked. It has come to my attention that you often engage in behavior that is meaningless, ridiculous, and unreasonable. Behavior which an outside observer might very well consider . . . stupid, to put it bluntly."

"I'll be derned." He sat up and began scratching his ear. "Are you sure it was me? That doesn't sound like anything I'd do."

"Of course I'm sure it was you, and it sounds *exactly* like something you would do. Shall we get down to specifics?" I began pacing back and forth in front of him. I often do this when . . . maybe I've mentioned that before. "Okay, I saw you snapping at that cottonwood cotton."

"Yep, that was me all right."

"I know it was you. That's my point. Do you realize how absurd you look when you do such things?"

"Not really."

"Well, you looked ridiculous and absurd. I mean, we are professional dogs, Drover. We hold important positions on this ranch."

"I didn't know I had a position."

"You don't, and one of the reasons you don't is that you're always doing something silly. If we gave you a position and a title, you'd embarrass the whole Security Division. Don't you understand that everything we do on this ranch must have a purpose?"

"I never thought about it . . . I guess."

"Well, it's time you thought about it." I stopped pacing and whirled around to face him. "What was your purpose in chasing those puffs of cotton?"

"Well, let me think. It was fun."

"Won't work, Drover. Having fun has nothing to do with our jobs. Having fun is for cats, chickens, ordinary mutts, and the other nitwits in this world. Try again."

"Well, let's see." He squinted one eye and drew his mouth up into a knot. He seemed to be concentrating. That was good. "I didn't want the cotton to litter the ranch . . . I guess."

"Litter the ranch?"

"Yeah. We're against litter, aren't we?"

I resumed my pacing. "Of course we're against

litter, but cottonwood trees are part of this ranch, and their seeds are part of the natural flauna and fluoride. That's not litter."

"Darn. Well, let me try again. I was hungry and wanted some cottonwood candy."

I stopped pacing and stared at the runt. "Cottonwood candy? I've never heard of such a thing."

"Well, it's like cotton candy, only it comes from cottonwood trees."

"No kidding?" I sat down. "Tell me more. This is something new."

"Well, let's see. Cottonwood candy comes from cottonwood trees . . . "

"You've already said that. Get on with it."

". . . and the best part is that you don't have to go to the circus to buy it."

"Hmm, yes, that fits. There are no circuses on this ranch." I began pacing again. This was starting to sound interesting. "Okay, Drover, we've got a lead here. We know for a fact that no circus has ever spent time on this ranch, yet you've reported finding traces of cottonwood candy. What made you think that the substance in the air was cottonwood candy rather than plain, ordinary cottonwood cotton?"

"'Cause I saw one in the air, and I chased it."

"Exactly, but what about the taste?"

"Well, it kind of rhymes with 'chase.'"

"Good point, and we may come back to that later. You see, Drover, candy, by its very nature, tastes sweet, and regular cotton candy is made up of equal parts of sugar and cotton. Therefore, it has a sweet taste. What about the stuff you snapped out of the air?"

"Well . . . it sure tasted like equal parts to me."

I whirled around with an air of triumph. "There we are! Do you understand what this means, Drover? We have made an amazing discovery. Those cottonwood trees down along the creek are producing *cottonwood candy*! They might have been doing this for centuries, but nobody ever knew it because nobody was ever bold or curious enough to taste one of the tiny fluffs of cotton until WE came along and did it."

Who's we?"

"We, Drover, the scientific division of the Security Division. We who dare to look foolish in the pursuit of our research."

"Yeah, but it was me that did it."

"Exactly. You played a small but tiny part in making this discovery, and you'll probably get some credit for it. But the important thing is that we have discovered an important new source of food and nourishment and . . ."

At that very moment, my eyes caught sight of a

small, white object floating through the air. It was a piece of cottonwood candy, and it was coming toward us.

"Okay, Drover, stand by. I'm going to demonstrate the proper technique for harvesting cottonwood candy. Watch this and take careful notes."

"I thought I already knew how."

"Your methods were crude, Drover. Not bad for a first attempt but a far cry from refined techniques. Watch."

I bent my knees and went into Stealthy Crouch Mode and waited until the candy puff was directly overhead. Then I hit the Launch Button, sprang upward, and snagged the luscious candy morsel in my jaws. I returned to earth and began smacking my lips on the . . .

SPUT! PATOOEY!

"Drover, you moron, that isn't sweet. It's nothing but a piece of fuzz."

"Well, I never said it was sweet. I said it tasted like equal parts, and you said . . ."

I didn't hear the rest of what he had to say, for at that very moment I became aware of a new and alarming sound behind me. I wheeled around and saw . . .

CHAPTER TWO

Mocked by the Small Minds on the Ranch

I saw Loper and Slim. They had come down from the house and were leaning on the legs of the gas tank. And the alarming sound I had heard was their laughter.

They appeared to be laughing at . . . something. I ran my gaze around in a full circle and saw nothing that might cause them such a fit of laughing. Then I heard them speak.

Slim: "Say, that's a pretty special dog you've got there. You reckon he's a registered hunter and jumper?"

Loper: "You bet. He hunts down cottonwood seeds and jumps to catch 'em. Sure makes me proud of my dog food bill."

Slim: "Why, yes. You know, Loper, them cotton

12

farmers down around Lubbock might pay big money for a dog like Hank. If you staked him out for twenty-four hours, I'll bet he might gather a whole bale of cotton."

Loper: "He sure might. Maybe I ought to get a patent on him."

Slim: "Boy, I would. Paint him green and put a John Deere sticker on him, and you might be able to rent him out by the month."

You can always spot the small minds in a crowd. They're the ones that laugh and hoot and ridicule anyone who's different, anyone who dares to experiment and push the outer limits of our scientific knowledge. And if history had been left to such hooters and scoffers, we'd still be . . . I don't know where we'd still be.

Yes I do. We'd still be living in a primitive state, without baling wire and zippers for blue jeans and better mousetraps. We'd have mice all over the place, eating up the world's supply of cheese, and those two jugheads would still be making jokes.

They think they're so funny. Well, they're not. If they didn't laugh at their own stale jokes, there would be a great silence every time they told one.

I held my head at a proud angle and gave them Poisonous Glares, just to let them know that all the great discoveries in science looked silly at first. My Poisonous Glares must have gotten to them—either that or they got so bored listening to each other, they couldn't stand it anymore—but whatever, at last they ran out of excuses for loitering and loafing.

Loper yawned and stretched. "Slim, why don't you load up some alfalfa on the flatbed and feed those momma cows in the Dutcher Creek pasture. They're chasing that early grass in the low spots, but they probably need a little extra protein. Feed the horse pasture and those yearlings in the south-east. Forty bales ought to be plenty."

Slim nodded. "Do I dare take the Cotton King with me?"

"Oh, I guess we can spare him, but be real careful. With this cattle market in the pits, we may need to branch out into the cotton business."

"I'll guard him with my life."

See? What did I tell you? They never quit. Well, if Slim thought I was going to help *him* feed hay, he was very muchly mistaken. I had better things to do—plenty of better things.

"Hank, come on! Load up."

No. I would not come on, and I would not load up.

Loper went down to the corrals or somewhere. I don't know where he went, nor did I care. Slim came walking toward me. I turned my eyes away and refused to look at him.

"Now Hankie, we were just funnin'. Don't be bitter."

Hey, I was bitter. Who wouldn't have been bitter? I had nothing more to say to Slim Chance, except that he wasn't nearly as funny as he thought. No, I would not come, and I intended to ignore him for days, maybe even weeks.

Dogs have feelings too. We can't be mocked and scorned day after day.

"Come on, Hankie. Let's go load some hay."

No. He could load his own hay, and he could do it alone, and after he'd spent a few weeks alone, without a loyal friend, maybe he'd learn to appreciate a good honest cowdog.

The Cotton King! I'd never been so insulted. If they had bothered to study the case, they would have known that the real so-called Cotton King on our outfit was Mister Squeakbox, who had invented the whole silly exercise.

I'd just been trying to help the little goof.

I should have known better. Helping Drover was Mission Impossible.

And no, I would not help Slim feed today, and maybe never again. My decision was final.

Slim shrugged and made his way to the flat-bed pickup in that slow walk of his. My glare followed him. It was a pity to end such a long friendship, but it couldn't be helped. He opened the door and reached inside. He came out with something in his hand. He took a bite of it and held it up.

"You want some beef jerky?"

My ears shot up and puddles of water began to form in my mouth. Well, I . . . I sure didn't want him thinking that all my anger and hurt and pain could be bought for one measly strip of beef jerky, but on the other hand . . . I, uh, found my steps taking me toward the pickup.

Don't get me wrong. I wasn't selling out one hundred percent. The pain and humilification would linger for weeks, and I would find it hard to hide the scars, but . . . well, beef jerky was a pretty good peace offering.

He tore off a hunk and pitched it into the air. You should have seen me snap that rascal! Snagged it out of thin air and gulped it down.

Old Slim chuckled at that. "Beats cotton, don't it?"

There for a moment I considered . . . oh well. Sticks and stones may break my bones, but beef will ease the pain. Someone on the ranch needed to show some maturity, and I figured it had to be me.

"You want to ride in the back or up front with the executives?"

Well, I had always enjoyed riding in the back and letting the wind blow my ears around, but . . . well, considering all the suffering I had endured that morning, maybe riding up front would be better. I leaped up onto the seat and took the Shotgun Position by the window.

Much to my surprise and dismay, Slim called Drover, and a moment later he joined me in the cab. I gave him a withering glare.

17

"Hi, Hank. Is something wrong?"

"Don't speak to me, you weasel. Of course something's wrong."

"Gosh, if I can't speak to you, how can I find out what's wrong?"

"You know what it is, and you were the cause of it. Once again, you have made a mockery of the entire Security Division."

"I thought we'd become famous scientists or something."

"We became famous idiots, Drover, and do you know why?"

"Not really."

"Because you told me a huge whopper of a lie and lured me into believing that story about cottonwood candy."

He grinned. "Oh yeah. That was quite a whopper, but I knew you'd never believe it."

"Yes, but I did believe it. I made the mistake of trusting you."

"That was a mistake."

"I just said that, and we don't need you repeating everything I say."

"What?"

"I said, we don't need me repeating everything you say."

"Oh, that's okay. I don't mind."

"And for telling huge whoppers to the Head of Ranch Security, you will be written up. I'm going to put three Shame-on-You's into your file."

"Oh drat."

"Make that four, Drover, since you've chosen to use naughty language while on duty. I hope this ruins your day and makes you feel lousy."

He grinned. "Yeah, it does."

"Then why are you grinning?"

"Well, let me think here." He rolled his eyes around. "I deserved it so much, the guilt feels good and makes me grin."

"Drover, that's the dumbest statement you've ever made."

"No, I said something dumber last week."

"What was it?"

"Well, it was so dumb, I tried to forget it, and now I can't remember."

"Shut up, Drover. Talking with you makes me feel insane."

I turned my gaze out the window and moved as far away from him as I could. Just sitting next to him scrambled my brain waves.

Slim fired up the motor, and we drove around to the stack lot, and in case you don't know, a stack lot is where we keep our stacks of alfalfa hay over the winter months. It's fenced off to keep the livestock...

Uh-oh. I saw the problem right away, even before Slim did. A bull had torn down the fence and had invaded the stack lot. No doubt he had been there most of the night, and he had wrecked the southwest corner of the stack.

Slim saw it too, and his eyes narrowed in anger. "Dadgum bull. Come on, Hank. We've got a job to do."

He flew out the door and opened the wire gate into the stack lot. I tried to follow him out the pickup door, but Drover was in my way. "Excuse me, but I've just been called out on a Code Three." He stared at me with empty eyes. "Will you please get out of my way?"

"When?"

"When what?"

"When did somebody get in your way?"

"*You're in my way right now!*"

"Oh my gosh, did something happen?"

"Yes, something happened. We're in a Code Three Situation. We're under Red Alert, and you're in my way, and I can't get out. Move!"

He moved, all right. He started turning circles right there in the seat. "Help, mayday, Red Alert, oh my leg!"

"Stop squeaking and spinning in circles! Jump out the door and attack that bull!"

"Bull? Oh my gosh, okay, here we go, out the door . . ."

At last he jumped out the door, but would you like to guess what he did the very instant his feet hit the ground? Instead of charging after the bull, he ducked under the pickup and hid. I couldn't believe it. I was so disgusted . . . oh well. I didn't have time to deal with Drover's problems.

I flew out the door and went ripping into the stack lot to give that smart-aleck bull a stiff dose of Ranch Justice. I'd never liked bulls in the first place, and I could hardly wait to tear this guy to shreds.

I Discover a Stray
Cat in the Haystack

By the time I reached the Combat Zone, Slim was already there. He'd found a piece of windmill rod, and he ran straight at the bull, yelling, waving his arms, and swinging the rod.

If he'd stopped to think about it, he might have tried a different approach. He got the bull so stirred up that, instead of stepping over the fence he'd already torn down, he tore out another six feet of posts and barbed wire. Then he headed west in a run.

Slim stopped, threw the windmill rod at him, and yelled, "You dadgum fence-wrecking bull! Get 'im, Hankie, and bite him twice for me!"

I zoomed past him and headed straight for the villainous bull. I threw all circuits over into Automatic and began the Targeting Procedure. Would you like to listen in? Okay, here's the conversation that was going on in the cockpit of my mind.

"Range...mark! Bearing...mark! All ahead two thirds, course two-five-zero! Open outer doors, flood tubes one and three, and plot a solution! We have a solution. Stand by to fire!"

Pretty impressive, huh? You bet it was. You probably thought we dogs just went out and barked at things. Ha! Far from it. Our Targeting Procedures are very precise and very complicated, and we have to...

HUH?

The bull had been, uh, running, don't you see, but all at once he stopped and wheeled around and . . . well, more or less turned back in my direction and . . . you must realize that all our calculations and Targeting So-Forths had been based on . . .

We had to, uh, plot a new solution, is the long and short of it. We went to Full Air Brakes, did a rapid turn to the starboard larboard, reversed directions, hit Full Flames on all engines, and went streaking back to the . . . well . . . to the pickup, you might say.

We needed some time to retarget, don't you see, and Data Control felt that Drover might need some help in . . . well, guarding the underside of the . . . we sure couldn't afford to lose that pickup.

I scrambled beneath the pickup and cut loose with a withering barrage of barking. Drover was there, his eyes as big as grapesfruit. Grapefruits, that is. "Did you get him?"

"Oh yeah, no problem. I don't think we'll see him again."

"Oh good. Boy, he sure was a big old bull."

I peeked out and saw that the bull was walking away. "He was nothing but a huge hamburger, Drover, and the bigger they are, the harder they cook." I noticed that he was staring at me. "Why are you staring at me?"

"Well, I don't know. Somehow that didn't make sense."

"Of course it made sense. The bigger they are, the . . . just skip it, Drover. I'm sorry I brought it up, and I don't have time to explain it. I've got work to do."

"Okay, I think I'll just stay here for a while. This derned old leg went out on me again."

"Yeah, I'll bet." I crawled out and gave the bull a few parting shots. "Let that be a lesson to you, you big galoot! Next time you won't be so lucky."

Pretty tough, huh? You have to be firm with these bulls.

I noticed that Slim was trying to patch up the fence, and I figured I'd better scoot over there and supervise. On my way across the stack lot, I caught sight of something out of the corner of my eye. It wasn't much, just a blur of color. Something was over there, and I needed to check it out.

I altered course and marched over to the spot. I stuck my nose between two bales of hay and . . . my goodness, it was a *cat*, a smallish, yellowish she-cat. My first instink was to raise all hackles and growl at her, which I did, but then I noticed that she had a more or less pleasant face, and she

didn't hiss at me or yowl. Still, she was a cat, and cats had no business on my outfit.

I mean, we already had one, and he was one too many. Pete, I mean. I had no use for Pete. He was lazy, hateful, spoiled, and constantly looking for ways of getting me into trouble. Have I mentioned that I don't like cats? I don't like cats, period.

"What are you doing in there?"

She spoke in a sad little voice. "I'm lost. I'm alone and abandoned. I need a home."

"Life is tough, ma'am. We have no homes for

cats. This is a cattle ranch, not a cat ranch. You're occupying my haystack and trespassing on my property. Oh yes, I'm Hank the Cowdog, Head of Ranch Security. You'll need to move along."

"But couldn't I stay in your haystack for a day or two?"

"No."

"I wouldn't be any trouble."

"Cats always cause trouble. The answer is no, I'm sorry. I'll be back here this afternoon to check things out. Nothing personal, ma'am, but you'd better be gone. Good luck."

I marched away from her. I kind of hated being so . . . hey, once you start boarding stray cats, there's no end to it. They'll move in and take over the place.

I joined Slim. I could see that he was experiencing a period of great darkness. He always does when there is a fence to repair. He doesn't enjoy fixing fence. I knew that about him and knew that in this hour of despair he needed a friend.

When I got there, he was standing over the wreckage, muttering to himself. "Of all the bum luck. I've got cattle to feed and hay to load, and that bull decides to wreck the stack lot fence."

I sat down beside him and struck a pose we call Loyal Friend Sharing Heartache. We save it for special occasions such as this one. Deep down, maybe I didn't really care all that much. I mean, there are many tragedies in the world that are worse than a trashed fence, but in the Ranch Dog Business, we get no points for bringing them up.

See, when our cowboys are depressed, they expect us to be depressed. When they're happy, they want us to be happy. That may sound a little strange, but that's what we dogs get paid for.

Slim shook his head and stared at the fence. He heaved a sigh. I followed his lead and did the same. We were both very depressed about this fence deal.

"I ain't got time to fix it right, plus I'm a little short on inspiration so I reckon I'll do a sharecropper patch and hope it'll turn a bull."

We had seen those sharecropper patches many times before. Slim and Loper were famous for their ingenuity in this department. They could take a stretch of old, rusted barbed wire and dinky posts, add some baling wire and a few staples, and make it just as sorry as it had been before.

Only this time, Slim added a new technique I hadn't seen before. Where the posts were broken off at the ground, he stood them up and wired in a crutch post on each side, making a kind of A-frame. It held up the fence, didn't cost the ranch any money in new material, and spared Slim the trouble of digging postholes.

I thought it was pretty clever. I also thought the bull would wreck it in about ten seconds, but of course I kept that thought to myself. These cowboys don't want advice from their dogs.

He spent fifteen minutes on it, and when he was done, he stood back and admired his work. "Well now, that ain't such a bad job, is it Hank?"

Uh . . . no. No, it was very nice. Beautiful. A fine piece of work. Too bad we didn't have a camera.

"I bet it'll turn that old bull, and if it don't, I've got a shotgun and some number seven loads that might get his attention. Come on, pooch, we've got hay to load and mouths to feed."

He crawled into the pickup and backed it up to the stack. You're probably wondering about Drover and if he got smushed, seeing as how he was still under the pickup, guarding the springs and shocks and U-joints. He didn't get smushed. He never gets smushed. He waited until the last possible second, then squirted out of danger.

Whilst Slim loaded the hay and stacked it on the flatbed, I threw myself into the task of ignoring Drover. He came up and started yapping about something or other, nothing that interested me in the least. I walked away in the middle of his so-called conversation and took up a new position. He followed and continued his yapping. At last I got tired of it.

"Drover, are you bored?"

"Who me? Well . . . yeah, maybe I am. How'd you know?"

"I always know when you're bored, because you start boring me with boring conversation."

"I'll be derned. I didn't know it was so obvious."

"It is. What you need is a little job to keep you busy, so why don't you walk over there to those two bales of hay—you see those two bales off to themselves? Walk over there, stick your head in between them, and bark as loud as you can."

"Okay, let's see if I can remember: two bales, stick my head, and bark. I think I've got it. But how come you want me to bark at the hay?"

"Just do it, Drover. For once in your life, follow an order and complete a task."

"Well . . . there's not a snake in there, is there?"

"No, there's no snake. You have my Cowdog Oath on it. Now go."

"Well, I guess . . . okay, here I go."

He went skipping over to the two bales of hay. I watched with great interest, heh heh, and had a fairly good idea what might happen. I didn't wish the dunce any trouble, but he needed some life experiences to occupy his tiny mind and to give him something new to talk about.

He reached the bales, looked back at me, and waved. I waved back. He stuck his nose in between the bales and did his best imitation of a deep roaring bark. It wasn't much of a bark, but it proved to be enough. Heh, heh.

He jumped three feet in the air and squalled, then came highballing it back to me. "Hank, there's a cat in there!"

"No kidding? A cat, huh?"

"Yeah, and I barked, and she slapped my face."

"Goodness. What a naughty cat. Why didn't you beat her up and run her off the ranch?"

"Well . . . I just couldn't do it. Who could beat up a cat with kittens?"

I stared into the huge vacuum of his eyes. "*What?*"

"Kittens. She's got six little baby kittens in there."

My eyes rolled back in my head. Oh great! We didn't have just one stray cat on the ranch. We had SIX! Seven, actually, if you counted the mother.

And guess who came slithering along at that very moment—speaking of stray and unwanted cats. It was Pete. No doubt he had heard the noise and had come to check it out. Oh, and he had been listening in on our conversation.

"Hi, Hankie. I hear we've got some new cats on the ranch."

I whirled around and showed him some fangs. "Get lost, Pete. The cats have to go. They're not staying on my ranch, and I don't want to hear what you have to say about it. I already know."

"I don't think you do, Hankie. It might surprise you."

"What are you saying, you little sneak? Out with it."

He blinked his eyes and grinned. "I think you should . . . order them off the ranch, right now. Throw them out. Make them leave. They don't belong here."

I stared into his cunning cattish eyes. He didn't know it, but he had just caused a train wreck in my mind. Suddenly I wasn't sure what kind of scheme he was trying to cook up. With cats, you never know. They say one thing, and it means something else, but you can always be sure they're up to no good.

Pete was up to no good, but I didn't have time to get to the bottom of his barrel. I had work to do, so I whirled around and marched away. But it continued to bother me. Only later did I discover why he had taken my side in the Stray Cat Debate.

CHAPTER FOUR

I Give Momma Cat the Order to Leave

We had stray cats on the ranch, but we wouldn't have them for long, not if I had anything to say about it.

I left Pete and Drover and marched straight over to the two bales of hay. I knocked on Madame Kitty's door—well, tapped on one of the bales, actually, since she didn't have a . . . I wanted to alert her to the fact that I was there to serve a warrant.

"Ma'am? Madame Kitty? Hello?"

She didn't answer. I heard only a bunch of little squeaks. I moved closer, so that I could peer into the space between the bales. There she was, stretched out on the ground with six kittens lined up along her belly.

I looked away. I mean, it didn't seem quite

proper for me to be invading her privacy and staring at her.

"Hello? I know you're in there. May I have a word with you?"

"I'm busy. Could you come back later?"

"I know you're busy, and no, I can't come back later. We have urgent business to discuss."

"Well . . . all right. Go ahead and talk. I can hear you. Just don't get too close."

"Oh? Why is that?"

"Well . . . I might have to knock your block off."

My ears perked up on that. "Knock my block off? Is that what you said? You, a shrimpy little cat who is breaking the law, might knock my block off? Ha! That's funny."

Her little voice reached my ears again. "I'm sorry to put it that way, but we mother cats have powerful reactions to dogs and loud noises. I don't want to do anything crazy."

"Oh, well good. I'd hate for you to do anything crazy."

"See, I slugged a dog just a few minutes ago. I didn't want to, but he stuck his nose in here and barked. He shouldn't have been here. He shouldn't have done that. I felt bad about it. Was he a friend of yours?"

"Uh . . . we're still debating that issue, ma'am.

34

We're not sure what he is, but I know the little mutt, yes."

"Please tell him I'm sorry, and please tell him not to do that again . . . or I'll have to knock his block off."

It was kind of funny, hearing such tough language from such a timid little cat. I enjoyed a private chuckle and then returned to the unpleasant business of being Head of Ranch Security.

I cleared my throat. "All right, ma'am, I'm here to inform you of your rights. You don't have any. I'm sorry you chose to bring your litter of kittens to my haystack, but you did, and now you have to leave."

There was a moment of silence. "But how can I leave?"

"I have no idea. No doubt it won't be easy, but surely you're not the first cat in history to face this challenge. You'll think of something. And just remember: this is your problem, not mine. I'm just doing my job. I'll be back in two or three hours. I sincerely hope that you'll be gone." Silence. "Hello? Did you hear me?"

"Yes sir. I'll do my best."

"Great. Doing our best is the best we can do. I wish you luck on your long journey away from here. Good-bye."

I marched away, feeling slightly . . . well, how

would you feel, ordering a scrawny mother cat and her six children off your place? It didn't make me real proud of myself, to be honest about it, but that's the price you pay for being Head of Ranch Security. This job is more than cookies and milk . . . sugar and spice . . . whatever.

Whatever it is, it's not always pleasant. But that was my problem, and I would have to figure out how to live with it. And I would.

I marched back to Drover. He had been watching, and he said, "What happened?"

"I told her to clear out. I told her that she can't keep her kittens on this ranch."

His eyes widened. "You told her that? That's awful!"

"What's awful about it? We're paid to enforce ranch law, Drover."

"Yeah, but she's a mother."

"Right. Every mother on earth is a mother. Your mother was a mother."

"Yeah, but . . ."

"If your mother had dumped a litter of kittens on this ranch, I would have thrown her off too."

"Yeah, but she never would have done that."

"Oh? What makes you so sure?"

"Well, she was a dog, and dogs can't have kittens."

I gave him a glare of purest steel. "Are you trying to make a mockery of this investigation? Do I need you to tell me that your mother couldn't have had kittens?"

"Well, I . . ."

"You take a mole and make a mountain out of it, Drover."

"No, she was a dog, just a plain old dog."

"What are you talking about?"

"My mother, dear old mom. She was just a dog."

"Of course she was a dog. What's your point?"

"You said she was a mole, but she wasn't." His lower lip began to tremble. "And I don't think it's very nice of you to say that she was a mole."

I took a deep breath of air, walked a few steps away, and tried to clear the sawdust and cobwebs out of my head. I looked up at the clouds. I studied the trees on the horizon. Only then did I return to Drover and his lunatic conversation.

"Let's start again, Drover. And just forget about your mother."

A tear slid down his cheek. "First you call her an ugly mole, then you tell me to forget about her. And now you're going to throw that poor little mother cat off the ranch! Sometimes I think you're just terrible!"

"Will you dry up? What's the big deal about the

cat? Have you forgotten that she slapped you on the nose?"

"Yeah, but I deserved it. If I'd been a mother cat and if I'd barked at my kittens, I would have slugged me too."

"Wait a second, hold it, halt. Say that again. I missed something."

"Well, let's see here." He sat down, hiked up his hind leg, and began scratching his left ear. I gave him a scowl.

"Must you scratch while we're talking?"

"It helps me think. Now let's see. If I were a cat with six little kittens . . . and then if I were a dog without any kittens . . ."

"Stop right there. If you were a cat, you couldn't be a dog."

"Yeah, but this is just plyke."

I stared into the vast emptiness of his eyes. "What is plyke?"

"Play-like, only you can shorten it to 'plyke' and save some time."

"I have a better idea for saving some time. Why don't you shut your trap and stop spreading chaos and confusion? You get me so messed up, I don't know whether it's raining or Tuesday."

"It's Wednesday."

"Hush, Drover, and let's get some work done. We have a ranch to run."

"Yeah, but my mother wasn't an ugly mole."

I heaved a sigh. "Okay, Drover, she wasn't a mole."

"Or ugly."

"She wasn't an ugly mole, and I never said she was, but never mind. Let's get back to work. And please hush."

"Okay."

"Thanks."

"You're welcome."

I hurried away before he could say anything that might send me over the edge of the brink.

You know, there are times when I think that Drover is really and truly . . . I don't even have a word for it, so let's just skip it.

Slim had just finished topping out his load of hay. He'd stacked it six high on the flatbed. It appeared to be a pretty decent job of stacking, but of course he would need to tie it down with a couple of ropes. I mean, that was a standard precaution we followed on the ranch. Driving over rough ranch roads, a guy could plant bales of hay in spots where he didn't want 'em to be.

Slim jumped down, dusted off his hands, and studied the load. "What do you think, pooch? Is that the best job of stacking you ever saw?"

It was a pretty good load, but it needed to be tied down.

"You know, I don't have any ropes with me. And you know what else?"

Our eyes met. I gave my tail Slow Wags, as if to say, "Surely you're not thinking..."

He grinned. "That's such a bodacious fine job of stacking, I think it'll ride all the way to the pasture without ropes."

See? I knew it! Too lazy to go back to the saddle shed for ropes.

"That'll make up for some of the time we wasted on that fence. Come on, pup. Load up, and let's get this show on the road."

Okay, fine. I'd tried to warn him, but had he listened? Oh no. Who was I, after all? Merely the Head of Ranch Security, just a dumb dog who happened to know quite a bit more about hauling hay than Mister Slim Chance did—and who could smell disaster in the wind.

You just wait and see what happened.

CHAPTER FIVE

Feeding Cattle with Slim Can Get Pretty Boring

Okay, maybe we didn't lose the load right away, but it was sheer good luck that kept it together, not Slim's stacking job.

And for the record, let me say that I watched it in the side mirrors as we drove along. You know that big pothole in the county road, just west of the . . . well, maybe you don't know it, since you've never . . . there was a big pothole in the caliche road, just west of the low-water crossing, and when we hit it with the right rear tire, I thought the load was going to quit us.

I watched in the mirror and held my breath. So did Slim. When it didn't fall, he winked at me

and grinned. "Heh. Solid as a brick wall."

Yeah, right. And when you're lucky, you don't need skill or brains.

We turned left onto the road, that led into the Dutcher Creek pasture and rumbled over the cattle-guard. I kept one eye on the mirror and one eye on Slim. The load held. Again, he gave me a wink and a grin.

I don't know why he had to make such a big deal out of it. Had we bet a large sum of money on it? No. I had merely expressed my opinion. And besides that, the day wasn't over. We still had several miles of ranch roads to cover on our feed run, and that right rear corner looked pretty cushy to me.

We passed Slim's house. Actually, it was a shack, a little cowcamp shack that showed the effects of being lived in by a bachelor cowboy. Does that make sense? Maybe not, so let me put it another way. If you'd been driving along, and somebody had pointed to Slim's place and said, "A bachelor cowboy lives there," you wouldn't have been surprised.

Fact One: The outside of the shack was decorated with black tar paper. Why? Because Slim and Loper had never gotten around to finishing it out with shingles or siding. They had begun the project years ago, but it had gotten derailed. What had been their excuse? "We'll finish it up when we get caught up on this ranch work," they had said.

Ha. They'd never caught up on the ranch work, and the outside of his shack had remained black and ugly. And you know what else? Slim couldn't have cared less. Black was probably his favorite color, if he had a favorite color . . . if he could even see color, and I'm not sure he could.

Fact Two: The curtains in the windows were the same curtains that had been there when he'd moved in, only now they were quite a bit dustier and fadeder . . . more faded, shall we say, than

43

before. I doubt that he'd ever touched them. I know for a fact that he'd never cleaned them. As far as I could tell, they served only one purpose—to hide the flyspecks on his windows and the piles of dead miller moths on the sills.

Fact Three: His yard showed all the love and care that a bachelor could give—none. There might have been five sprigs of buffalo grass in that yard, but mostly it was Russian thistles, soapweed, sunflowers, cockleburs, and gourd vines. When strangers came to visit—about once every two years—they often pointed to the gourd vines and said, "My, your watermelons are doing great!" And Slim would say, "Yup, but I have to work at it."

Right. I happen to know that in five years, Slim had spaded up his yard three times. How do I know that? Because that's the number of times his sewer had stopped up, and he'd had to turn some dirt to reach the cleanout.

Oh, and have we mentioned his flowers? He had flowers in the yard. There was one little patch of iris on the south side of the house. They'd probably been there for fifty years and had somehow managed to survive. I don't know if they ever bloomed. If they did, he'd probably rush out and spray them with poison to keep them from messing up his tar paper color scheme.

Fact Four: He had a clothesline in the back yard. The posts were made of old four-by-four timbers, with two-by-four crossarms. They'd probably been put there by buffalo hunters in the 1870s, and they looked like two Old Rugged Crosses with one strand of galvanized wire strung between them.

And as you may know, his clothesline was always loaded down with clothes. This might have fooled some people into thinking that Slim was neat and clean. That's a laugh. We dogs knew the true story. He "warshed" his clothes maybe once a month, then left them flapping on the line so he wouldn't have to fold them or put them in a drawer.

Anyways, that was Slim's shack, and we drove past it on the way to feed the Dutcher Creek cows. Slim guided the pickup down a little hill and parked in a grassy flat west of the creek. There, he honked the horn and called the cows in his usual manner—by cupping his right hand around his mouth and yelling, "Wooooooo! Wooooooo cow!" His cow calling always hurt my ears, and it always caused his Adam's apple to jump around.

Whilst we waited for the cows to come in, he picked through the litter on the floor of the pickup and came up with an old, yellow copy of the *Twitchell Picayune*. Does anybody know what a picayune is or why it became the name of a news-paper? Not me.

Anyways, he found the paper and began reading it. I don't know why he bothered. It was the same paper he'd been carrying around and reading for two months. Oh, and it had an oil stain on the front page where he'd used it to clean his dipstick. That was the one day he hadn't used my ear.

He scrunched down in the seat, tipped the brim of his hat down to his nose, propped the paper on the steering wheel, and began reading—to me, it seemed, as though I were interested, which I wasn't.

"Huh. Get this. Penny Scribner had triplets. That'll keep old Johnny busy, trying to feed all them hungry babies." He read some more. "I'll be derned. The Baptist ladies are having a bake sale. I'll bet it's a good 'un. Them old gals can sure cook." He rattled the paper and turned to an inside page. "Hey, get a load of this classified ad: 'To the owner of the ugly black dog. Your dog killed three of my laying hens last Thursday. If you don't tie him up, I will, and his feet won't touch the ground. Signed, Bobby Barnett.'"

He turned to the back page. I watched as he squinted his eyes, changed the angle of his head, and moved the paper around. "Either they smudged the ink on this thing or I'm going blind. I may be

forced to go to the dime store and try on their bifocals, if they ever put 'em on sale. You reckon bifocals would spoil my good looks?"

Suddenly I realized that he was staring at me. What was the question? My mind had, uh, wandered, it seemed.

"Hank, if you don't start paying closer attention to this conversation, I'm liable to get my feelings hurt and quit talking." He went back to the paper. "A lot of dogs would give anything to feed cattle with me and listen to my sparklin' conversation. Say, listen to this. Texas leads the nation in the production of bat manure. A guy never knows what he'll learn, readin' the *Picayune*."

He folded it up and laid it back on the floorboard. I blinked my eyes and yawned. I had spent more exciting times watching ants. I guess he noticed.

"What's the deal? You bored?"

Yes, as a matter of fact.

"You want me to sing you a song?"

No. Thank you.

"Okay, since you asked, since you be pleaded, since you love my singin', and got such great taste in music, I'll sing But just one. Don't ask for two."

Oh brother.

Well, here's what he did .

Slim's Boring Song

There was a handsome cowboy who lived
    all alone
In a tar paper shack he'd made into a home.
The ladies all loved him and banged on his door
But he sent 'em away and made 'em all cry in
    their sorrow.

It wasn't because he didn't like pretty
    wimmenin
Or thought he didn't need the touch of the
    feminine.
He did and he knew it, 'cause his shack was
    a mess,
But he was deeply devoted to his best pal
    named Hankie the Wonderdog.

Yippy ti-yi-yo, stay awake, little doggy,
I wish you could sing, but I know that you
    cain't.
Yippy ti-yi-yo, stay awake, little doggy,
The sunshine is bright, but I know that
    you ain't.

Now, Hank and his master fed cattle all day,
Hauled truckloads and truckloads of alfalfa hay.

Come evening, they found theirselves back at
the house.
Slim cooked 'em a supper of steak and lobster
and green beans.

And then they sat down for an evening of fun.
Slim read him the *Picayune* 'til a quarter to
one.
Hank begged him to sing with his wonderful
voice,
So he sang many songs, and Hank really
loved 'em a whole bunch.

Yippy ti-yi-yo, stay awake, little doggy,
I wish you could sing, but I know that
you cain't.
Yippy ti-yi-yo, stay awake, little doggy,
The sunshine is bright, but I know that
you ain't.
The sunshine is bright, Hank, but I know
that you ain't.

He finished his so-called song and gave me a big
grin. "Well, what do you think of that one, Hankie
boy?"

I thought . . . I thought it was about the DUMB-
EST song I'd ever heard. Not only was it incorrect

and full of baloney, but half of his lines didn't even rhyme. Furthermore, it was clear to me that Slim needed to find a job that gave him less idle time.

Oh, and I'd heard the part about "The sunshine is bright, but I know that you ain't." Not funny, not funny at all.

But of course he got a big chuckle out of it. "Yep, you're a very lucky dog, Hank. Not only do I read the paper to you, but I write songs for you and perform 'em, live and in person. Sometimes I wonder, though, if you really appreciate all the swell things I do for you."

Well, I could clear that up right away. I didn't appreciate any of it. His paper-reading-aloud was totally boring, and his singing reminded me of a windmill that needed grease. And next time he wanted me to go feed with him, I would stay home.

He yawned and looked out the window. "Well, looks like we've got the cows. Reckon they came up to hear my singin'?" He rolled up his window. "Better shut this winder or I'll get alfalfa leaves in this pretty pickup." He started the motor, put her in compound, let out on the clutch, opened the door, and stepped out. "Well, pooch, I'll throw off the hay, and you can drive."

He slammed the door and left me alone in the moving pickup.

CHAPTER SIX

Beware: This Chapter Is Very Scary

Are you shocked that Slim would step out of a moving pickup and leave me alone in the cab? It sounds pretty dangerous, but it really wasn't. We did it all the time, Slim and I.

See, when two men feed hay, one drives while the other cuts the wires on the bales and throws the hay off on the ground. When only one guy feeds, he puts the pickup in the slowest gear, climbs up on top of the load, and does the so-forth. The purpose of this procedure is to make sure the hay gets scattered over a long line. If you don't scatter the hay, the biggest cows and the ones with horns will end up with all the grub.

You're probably amazed that a dog would know so much about the business of feeding hay to livestock. Well, I have to admit that it's pretty amazing, but it's the sort of thing a Head of Ranch Security has to know about and understand. A lot of your ordinary ranch mutts pay no attention to such matters. They just sit there in the pickup, looking out the window and saying, "Duh." Or they sleep.

Drover sleeps. He knows nothing about haying livestock, even though he's spent most of his life on a ranch, and the reason is that he sleeps all the time and doesn't pay attention. It hurts me to say that about Drover, but it's true.

Oh, and one more thing about the Moving Pickup Maneuver: it only works if you have a wide, flat area, a feed ground, as we call it. If you're in rough country, with hills and ravines and canyons, you can get yourself into a world of trouble. I guess you can see why. It wouldn't be funny if the pickup ran off a cliff whilst the driver was up on top of the hay.

But never fear. We had us a nice, flat feed ground just west of the creek. There was no chance of the pickup running amuck. On flat ground, it steered itself, don't you see, and if it ever started heading toward the creek, Slim would jump down and steer it back on course. Or . . .

Hmmm. I had never actually tried to steer the pickup myself. I mean, that would have been asking a lot of a dog, even a Head of Ranch Security, but what was the big deal about steering a pickup?

Heck, Little Alfred was steering the pickup for his daddy when he was three years old.

When Alfred was three years old, not Loper. When Loper was three years old, Alfred was just a baby. No, wait. When Loper was three years old, Alfred wasn't even born.

Okay, but the point is that steering a slow-moving pickup was no big deal, and I had a feeling that if Slim or Loper ever asked me to do it, I could handle it. All you have to do is keep her between the ditches, as they say. Or to bring it closer to home, keep her out of canyons and creek bottoms.

Anyways, the pickup was chugging along in first gear, which we ranch dogs refer to as grandma-low or granny-low or grandma or granny or sometimes compound. Why do we call it compound? I have no idea.

I sat up in the seat and watched the scenery up ahead. Through the side mirrors, I couldn't see Slim, but I could see the signs of his work: alfalfa leaves flying around in the wind and blocks of hay landing on the ground.

He was busy. That was good. Maybe it would take his mind off of singing.

I must admit that it made me feel kind of important, sitting up there in the seat of that big old pickup, all by myself, the only dog within miles. I mean, it was kind of like . . . well, being the captain of a steamboat or a battleship or something. You're the only dog on the bridge (that's what they call the cab of a ship: a bridge). Anyways, you're the only so-forth, and you look through the windows at the vast ocean in front of you and . . .

Well, you can steer the ship, if you want. The wheel is right there in the bridge, and all you have to do to steer that huge ship and make it change course is . . . well, place one paw on the wheel and push down. Which I did, and sure enough, the ship . . . pickup, actually . . . the ship changed course to the right.

Or to the starboard bow, as we ship captains call it. See, in the steamboat and battleship business, we never say left or right. That would be too common, and we don't use common terms. We say starboard and . . .

Where did that big rock come from? There was a big rock dead ahead, and I was pretty sure it hadn't been there just a minute before. Or if it was, I hadn't seen it, and although it wasn't a huge rock, it was pretty big.

No problem. Ship captains encounter rocks all the time; also islands, ice cubes, and choral reeps. Icebergs, not ice cubes. An ice cube would be no sweat. Say, that's kind of a play on words, isn't it?

An ice cube is no sweat. Get it? Heh. I get a kick out of messing around with words and . . .

BUMP!

Oh yeah, the rock. Well, what can I say? I'd gotten all wrapped up in the excitement of being the captain of a naval battleship and had more or less forgotten to steer a course around the rock. No problem. The ship went over it . . . the pickup went over it, shall we say, and while it caused us to bump and lurch from side to side, we came through it with smiling colors.

Flying colors, I guess it should be. We came through the scary ordeal with flying colors. In fact, it was kind of fun. Calm seas are nice for some people and dogs, but those of us with a taste for adventure and danger . . .

I froze. My eyes were locked on the right side mirror. Why had Slim thrown off that big pile of bales in one spot? I mean, the whole purpose of feeding hay from a moving vehicle was to scatter it out, right? So why had he dumped . . . my goodness, there must have been ten bales on the ground.

Well, I would have to talk to Slim about this. I knew he was impatient sometimes and had a tendency to be . . . how can I put this? Might as well just blurt it out. He had a tendency to be lazy, and no doubt he'd gotten lazy and had dumped a bunch of bales on the ground in one spot. Well, there was no excuse for that. If you're going to do a job, you might as well . . .

There was a leg sticking out of those bales.

I'm not kidding. I saw it with my own eyes, in the mirror on the right side of the pickup. It appeared to be a human leg with a boot on the end of it. And an arm? A human arm?

Dear gussy, this was a real puzzler. Who or whom could that be? I mean, when you see an arm and a leg, you naturally assume that . . . well, you assume there's more. Other body parts. A person. Hmmm.

Okay, a pattern began to develop here. Some unknown person had been walking around in our Dutcher Creek pasture. Why? We still didn't know. And another thing we didn't know was why Slim had decided to dump about ten bales of hay on him.

Wait, hold everything! Remember that rock? You'd probably forgotten about it, right? Well, we ran over a rock, which caused the pickup to lurch

and . . . it's coming fast now, so hang on. Remember what I said about tying down the load with ropes? Slim chose not to do it, right? And remember my observation that the right rear corner of the load appeared to be cushy?

Ha! Well, guess what. Just as we'd passed that stranger in the pasture, the pickup had lurched over the rock, causing the load to shift suddenly to one side and spilling twenty bales on top of the poor hapless stranger.

There you are. The mystery was solved, and guess who had predicted it. Not Slim, fellers. It was ME. I had known . . .

Wait a minute. What were the chances of encountering a total stranger in the Dutcher Creek pasture? And what were the chances that our load of hay would fall on top of him, burying every part of him but one arm and one leg?

Not great. No chance at all. Out of the question. Okay, so whose arm and leg . . . I stared into the side mirror. A head appeared from the rubble of hay bales. I recognized the head. It belonged to . . .

Slim?

I'm sorry, but I broke into a fit of uncontrollable laughter. I know it's tacky to laugh at the misfortunes of others, but think about it. It was so fitting, so right, so heavy with justice and irony. I mean, here was the guy who'd been too lazy to tie down his load with ropes, right? Who'd been warned by the Head of Ranch Security that we might lose the load, right?

Well, by George, the chickens had come home to rot. Old Shin had chosen to do a sloppy job, and he'd gotten buried by his own load of hay. That was rich. I loved it! I could hardly wait to hear what he had to . . .

HUH?

Wait a minute. If Slim was back there, climbing out from under his stacking job, and if I was sitting in the seat of a moving . . .

My eyes swung around to the front. We were heading straight for the creek bank.

Gulk.

Okay, I'd seen just about enough. I hit the button for Major Alarm. "Attention all hands. This is your captain squeaking. Speaking, that is. We have veered off course and are heading for a disaster. Therefore, as your captain, I am giving the order to abandon ship. At the end of this message, I will dive out the window. I urge the rest of you to save yourselves. Thanks for your loyal service and courage in the face of a crisis. Until we meet again . . . good luck, men."

I signed off and glanced around the ship that had been my home upon the waters for so many months and years. Then, with a heavy heart, I went into a deep crouch and sprang upward and outward, toward the vast sea from which we all . . .

BONK!

Was this a joke? Someone had . . . somehow the window had . . . and then I remembered, and the total reality of my situation came crashing down upon me.

Slim had rolled up the dadgum window. I was

trapped inside a moving pickup that was . . . yikes . . . headed straight for the creek bank!

Okay, this called for drastic measures. I had no choice but to hurl the full weight of my enormous body against the window and destroy it in a crash of flying glass. I hated to do that to Slim's pickup, but . . . hey, was I going to ride that sucker all the way down into the bottomless waters of Wolf Creek?

No way, Charlie. I was getting out of there.

I took three deep breaths, loosened up the muscles in my soldiers, and prepared my mental energies for an emergency procedure we call Doggie Battering Ram. We very seldom use it and very seldom need it. Now . . . we needed it.

And so it was that, after preparing myself mentally and physically for this dangerous escape procedure, I coiled my legs under me, hurled myself like a cannonball at the window, and . . .

BONK!

Holy smokes, I was trapped inside a runaway pickup!

CHAPTER SEVEN

The Runaway Pickup Plunges into the Bottomless Creek

Pretty scary, huh? Yes, I had found myself in many scary and dangerous situations in my career, but this one may have been the very worst.

Just think about it. I was locked up in a sealed runaway pickup, which was heading for the bottomless waters of Wolf Creek, and the only guy who could save me was buried under twenty bales of alfalfa hay.

I'm not sure you'll want to go on reading. This could get bad. It could get so bad and so scary, it might stunt your growth or . . . I don't know, cause you to break out in warts or something. Use your own judgment. If you don't think you can handle it, just put the book away and find something else to do. Never mind that you'll be turning your back on a friend and leaving me all alone in my moment of greatest need.

Maybe you can find another friend. If you do, I hope you'll treat him better than you've treated me and that you'll stand by him through thick and thicker.

Or maybe you'll keep on reading, and we'll ride this thing down together, friends to the bitter end. That would be the only decent thing to do, and it's the sort of thing you'd expect a *real* friend to do. But, as I say, you'll have to make up your own mind. Don't let anything I've said influence your decision.

It's a free country, and you're old enough now to start making decisions for yourself. If you want to be a scrounge, a quitter, a backstabber, and a total bum, I guess you can leave.

But I don't have that option. I have to get back to the story. Are you with me or not? Okay, let's get on with it.

Things looked bad, real bad. You want to know how bad they were? Through the windshield, I could see two big birds circling above me. Would you care to guess what kind of birds they were? Not crows, not starlings or blackbirds or swallows. No sir. They were *buzzards*, and you might recall that ancient piece of cowdog wisdom that states, "When buzzards show up, fellers, it's usually a bad almond."

Omen. Whatever. It's a bad sign.

And there they were, circling overhead, and I even recognized them. Wallace and Junior. Those guys had followed me around for years, hoping that someday I might fit into their dinner plans, and here they were again—and this time, they just might get their wishbone.

They wheeled around in the air for a while. Then one of them—Wallace, it turned out—came swooping down, buzzed the pickup, so to speak (a buzzard buzzing the pickup, get it?), and came within inches of hitting it. He came so close, in fact, that he clipped the radio antenna and broke it off. No kidding.

Well, it wasn't actually an antenna, not the kind you buy in the store. Slim had busted off the real antenna about six months before. He'd run into a tree limb or something, and that had left him with a stub and no radio reception. So he'd rigged up his own. Would you like to guess what it was? A metal coat hanger, fastened to the stub with baling wire.

It was a typical Slim fix-up deal—ugly, tasteless, and tacky—but you know what? It worked, but that was before it got clipped off by a swooping buzzard.

Anyways, Wallace swooped past the windshield and clipped the antenna, and as he passed, I saw that he had a wild, joyful expression on his ugly beaked face, and I heard him yell, "Hi puppy dog. Me and Junior'll be standing by for rescue work. Adios!" And then he swope away.

Swoped. Swopen. Swoopen. Do I care?

Well, seeing hungry buzzards in the sky didn't give me a great feeling of confidence about this deal, but it did make me wonder how those guys always managed to show up in the darkest of moments. I don't have much good to say about buzzards, but you've got to admit that they're geniuses when it comes to smelling disaster.

Gulp. And it appeared that I had one in progress. I was sealed in a Ford F-250 casket and was chugging toward the creek. There was no escape, no hope, no solution. What did I do? I did what any normal, healthy cowdog would do.

I began chewing on the steering wheel.

At first glance, you might think that was a dopey thing to do. How could it help? Well . . . I'm not sure. All I can tell you is that, amongst us dogs, it's a normal and healthy response. When scared beyond recognition, we start chewing on the first object we encounter. In my case, it happened to be the steering wheel.

I don't think there's anything special, or magical about steering wheels. When they're handy, we chew 'em, that's all. And can testify that it made me feel better. It sort of took my mind off my problems as I chug, chug, chugged toward the creek.

I knew Slim would understand. After, they sent down the divers to find the pickup, after they hooked the winchline onto the back bumper and hauled it out on dry land, he would open the door and find my lifeless carcass, and there beside me would be the chewed-up steering wheel. And through his tears of grief, he would say, "Well, I reckon it brought a little aid and comfort to my pal Hank in his last hour, so it went to a worthy cause."

Pretty sad, huh? But I'll tell you something about steering wheels. They're hard to chew, and they don't taste so great. If I'd had it all to do over again, I might have chewed something softer, such as the seats.

Well, we've put this off as long as we can. Sooner or later we've got to come to the bad part, when the pickup finally goes over the bank and into the creek. Are you ready? I guess I'm ready. Thanks for sticking with me. Thanks for all the memories. Thanks for helping me chew the steering wheel.

I held my head at a proud angle, and like a ship's captain about to go down with the ship, I . . .

Who would have thought that this particular stretch of Wolf Creek was only about six inches deep? Not me. Heck, I'd supposed it was, oh, fifty, sixty feet deep at least. It *looked* deep. Okay, maybe it didn't look all that deep, but who notices such tiny details when he's sitting in the cab of a runaway pickup? And chewing the steering wheel? Not me.

And I'll guarantee you that Drover wouldn't have noticed. Why, if he'd been in there with me, he'd have . . . I don't know what he'd have done, but it would have been loud and weird.

Okay, let's wrap this thing up. The pickup chugged up to the creek bank and went plunging over the brink of the edge. You probably thought it would be a sheer drop-off of thirty or forty feet, but it was more on the order of . . . well, two or three feet, but it was a sheer drop, and it did rattle my teeth. (I had a hard bite on the steering wheel, don't you see.)

Once in the creek bed, the pickup continued chugging forward, out into the water, which you thought was bottomless but which turned out to be only six inches deep. Or maybe four. It was deep enough so that I saw three minnows and a water spider swimming along.

Pretty shallow, actually, and the pickup moved across the creek until it came to a tree, and there it quit moving. And then the motor died. Whew!

An eerie silence moved into the cab. I glanced around and realized that I was alive and in one piece. What amazing good luck! By George, I had ridden that speeding runaway pickup right up to Death's Doorknob and had lived to tell the story.

Hmmm. The steering wheel showed some signs of, uh, heavy use, shall we say, and that might take some explaining. Or if I was lucky, maybe Slim wouldn't notice. Or through wags and sad looks,

I might be able to convince him that ... well, termites had done it.

Anything could chew up a steering wheel, not
just dogs. And sometimes they just fall apart. No
kidding. Happens all the time.

Speaking of Slim, at that very moment he came
running up. I guess he'd worked his way out from
under that pile of hay and had come streaking after
the pickup to save ... well, ME, you might say, his
loyal dog. He was huffing and puffing, and his face
was bright red from all the exertion. See, Slim
wasn't exactly an Olympic champion when it came
to running. His usual mode of moving was a slow
slouch.

Anyways, he ripped open the door, and his whole
face brightened with relief. I could see, it in his eyes,
in his smile, everything. The guy was so glad and
happy, I found it a little embarrassing, to tell you
the truth. And then he spoke.

"Hankie boy, we sure come through this deal
smellin' like a rose. I was scared my spit can might
have turned over on the dash."

HUH?

Spit can? I followed his gaze to the tuna fish
can on the dash. Sure enough, it hadn't turned over,
but was that a big deal? Hey, I had just ... I don't

know what a dog has to do around here to . . . phooey. Skip it.

I knew that deep in his heart, Slim was very glad to find me alive and unharmed, and I was pretty happy about that myself. I went to Wild Joyful Wags on the tail section and threw myself into his awaiting arms and began licking him on the face and ears.

He laughed and patted me on the back. "Were you scared, pooch? I'll bet you were. That was a pretty scary deal. You know, all these years I've been feedin' hay by myself, I've wondered what might happen if a guy fell off the load. I reckon we found out, didn't we? And you can stop lickin' me any time now. Quit!"

He pushed me away. It was then that his eyes fell upon . . . well, upon the chips and sawdust, you might say, and the various parts of the . . . uh . . . steering wheel. There was a long moment of silence. Then . . .

"Good honk, what happened to my steering wheel?"

Well, I . . . in my hour of greatest need . . . in the terror of the moment, don't you see, I had felt this need to . . . dogs often do odd and peculiar things when . . .

All at once I was overcome by the feeling that I

was trying to explain something that couldn't be explained.

I lowered my head, tucked my tail between my legs, and moved as far away from him as I could, which placed me over against the door handle on the right side of the cab. There, I beamed him several different expressions, which included Awkward Grins, Funeral Home Eyes, and another one that attempted to say, "I know nothing about this, no kidding. It wasn't me. Maybe you have . . . termites . . ."

Then our eyes met. In the great gulf of silence that loomed between us, I waited to hear his next words.

CHAPTER EIGHT

Slim's Mackerel Sandwiches Are Poisonous

His next words came as a shock to me. I had expected that he might call me a few names and throw a hissy fit.

That's not what happened.

Here's what happened. His face collapsed into a scowl, and he had just opened his mouth, as if to deliver me a lecture on why dogs shouldn't chew steering wheels, when suddenly his eyes moved from me to a . . .

Hmmm. What was that? It appeared to be a spot on the seat, a . . . uh . . . rather large wet spot on the . . . on the driver's side, about where he usually . . . sat, you might say.

Slim, that is. Where he usually sat on the seat. Oops.

His face turned red. His eyes widened, then narrowed into angry squints. His nostrils flared.

His eyes came at me like bullets. "What's that?"

I had no idea. Honest. No kidding. This was the first I'd seen of it. Okay, I had some idea. It was a wet spot. A spot of wetness.

Rain. It had rained, and the window had been . . . wait, the window had been rolled up, right? So maybe the roof had, uh, leaked. Yes, that was it. A leaky roof.

Yikes, his face was getting redder by the second. This was looking bad, very bad. I glanced around, hoping to find a trap door or secret passageway that might let me out of there. No luck. At that point, I began to consider the pros and cons of hurling myself through the window, but no, I had already tried that deal.

Gulp. Once again I was trapped, and his eyes were burning holes in me. I couldn't look at him. I mean, I knew nothing, almost nothing about the wet spot on the seat, but still, I felt terrible about it, and well, the evidence did look pretty bad.

He was mad, really steamed. I counted my heartbeats and waited for the storm to hit. At last he spoke.

"Hank, have you ever been beat to death with a ballpeen hammer?"

Uh . . . no, never.

"Has anybody ever tied you up in a gunnysack and throwed you into a pit full of alligators?"

Not that I could, uh, recall. No.

"Well, somebody should have done it a long time ago, and the only reason they didn't was they didn't want to waste a good gunnysack." He kicked the side of the pickup. "You're worthless, dumb as a box of rocks." He kicked the pickup again. "First you chewed up my steering wheel, and then you puddled all over my seat. Didn't you?"

I . . . but you see . . . okay, yes, I'd done it. I was a rat and a bum, and he might as well fetch the hammer and get on with the ugly business.

He glared at me through his glasses—which, by the way, were speckled with green bits of alfalfa hay. He glared at me and shook his head and muttered words under his breath.

How was I supposed to respond to that? When they don't come right out and say what's on their minds, how can a dog . . . I mean, communication is impossible without communication, right? When they just stand there, moving their lips and muttering under their breath . . .

At last he broke the awful silence. "Hank, you're

74

so dumb it hurts. But you know what hurts even worse?"

No, I had no idea. And I wasn't sure I wanted to know.

He leaned into the cab and brought his face right up to mine. "What hurts even worse is that I may be even dumber than you are, since I'm the dufus that caused it all."

I stared at him in disbelief and even dared to tap the end of my tail.

"If I'd tied down the dadgum hay with ropes, like you're supposed to, none of this would have happened." Yes, I had tried to warn him about that. "And if a man ain't smarter than his dog, I guess he gets what he deserves—a chewed-up steering wheel, a seat that's been pottied on, and a pickup sitting in the middle of the dadgum creek."

He leaned against the side of the pickup, snatched his hat off his head, and used it to fan his face. "Boy, this day ain't going according to plan." He heaved a sigh and looked down at his feet. "Well, here I am, standing in the creek, and I notice that my boots leak. Is there anything else we can do to foul up the day? Yes, there is. We could be stuck, and then I could have the pleasure of walkin' back to headquarters in wet boots and explaining to the boss how I happened to park his pickup in the creek."

He climbed into the cab and slammed the door. Perhaps he had already forgotten about the wet spot on the seat, and I sure wasn't going to bring it up.

"Well, I reckon we'd better find out if we're stuck or not."

He fired up the motor, stomped on the gas, threw her into reverse, and popped the clutch. We lurched backward a few feet, and yes, I did go sailing into the dashboard. Slim got a chuckle out of that and said, "Hang on, pooch, 'cause Barney Oilfield is at the controls." He shifted into grandma-low, popped the clutch, and threw me back into the seat.

He repeated this several times, back and forth, until at last he plowed his way up the west bank and back on dry land. I had never met Barney Oilfield, but he must have been a crazy driver. But the important thing was that we had rescued the pickup, and that left Slim in a much better mood.

He grinned down at me. "You know, Hank, you're so graceful, maybe we ought to be sending you to ballet school."

Ballet school? What did that mean? I didn't know if this was a sincere compliment or just another of his cowboy jokes. With these guys, you never know. But his smile soon faded, and he snapped his finger.

"Dern. I've got to load all them bales back on the flatbed."

We pulled around to the pile of bales, and with much grunting and muttering, he reloaded the hay. I supervised the loading process and checked for mice beneath the bales. (No mice, and he did a pretty fair job of stacking.)

That done, we went on with our feed run and pitched out hay to the cows on down the creek. At twelve o'clock, we found ourselves in the East Creek pasture, far from home and food, but Slim had come prepared. He drove under a big cottonwood tree, shut off the motor, and reached into the glove box. He pulled out a brown paper sack, which . . . hmmm, had a pretty interesting smell about it.

He must have noticed that I had noticed. "Heh. You didn't know you was here in the cab with my dinner, did you? Heh. It's a good thing you didn't. Old Slim'll overlook a few fangmarks on the steering wheel, but don't be messin' with his dinner."

Well, no, of course. I knew that, and if he thought . . . hmmm. It did smell pretty yummy, and yes, it was a good thing I hadn't known it was in there.

It appeared to be a sandwich. He had wrapped it in . . . was that newspaper? Yes, by George, he had wrapped his sandwich in a piece of newspaper. He removed the newspaper, held the sandwich in his hands, and admired it. He smelled it and cut his eyes toward me. He might have noticed that I was . . . well, watching. Watching with considerable interest. My ears leaped up, and I licked my chops.

Yes, I'm sure he noticed, because he gave me a big grin. "Now, ain't this a beautiful samwitch? Built it myself. Canned mackerel and taco sauce. It's my own recipe." He took a big bite. Red juice oozed out of the sides—taco sauce, I guess it was—and dripped onto his fingers and jeans. He licked his fingers and then waved the sandwich under my nose. "Here, I reckon I can spare you a smell."

You probably think that I tried to steal a bite of it, but I didn't. No, if he'd wanted me to join him for lunch, he would have brought me something. I was sorry he didn't consider our friendship worth a sandwich or some token reward, but apparently he didn't and that was fine.

It smelled pretty good. Not great, but pretty good. I'd never been wild about the smell or taste of canned mackerel. At certain times of certain days, I'd even gone on record as saying that mackerel stinks. But on this particular day, as we were picnicking under the cottonwoods, it didn't smell half bad.

Pretty good, actually, and the longer I sat there watching, him eat and listening to him slurp and smack, the better it smelled. I might have preferred roast beef or fried steak, but those items weren't on the menu.

He waved it under my nose again. Why was he doing this? I mean, it's not polite to eat in front of your friends, right? Even dogs know that, yet here he was, not merely eating in front of his loyal friend and hay-hauling partner but also waving the sandwich in front of my nose.

And by the way, it smelled *great*. I've always loved the aroma of fresh canned mackerel. The taco sauce I can take or leave, but mackerel? Great smell. It always reminds me of ocean spray and enchanted islands and . . . well, food.

I was pretty sure that he would offer me a bite. That would be the polite and mannerly thing to do, and to encourage his manners and politeness, I swept the pickup seat with broad wags of my tail and showed him, through perked ears and facial expressions, that I was ready for my portion.

I waited. He took another bite. He gave me a wink. What was the deal? Surely he wasn't going to eat it down to a stub and give me the crusts. I mean, he'd done that before. Did he think I had some special fondness for crusts of bread? Hey, if he didn't want to eat them, why should I?

No thanks. If it was a mackerel sandwich, I wanted some mackerel.

At that very moment, he saw something out of the corner of his eye. He turned his head to the left and said, "I'll be derned. There's that same road-runner I seen over here just the other..."

SNAP!

Well, what did he expect me to do? Sit there like a "box of rocks" (his term) whilst he slobbered

and smacked and showed terrible manners and devoured our whole mackerel sandwich? Heck no. I did what any normal, healthy American dog would have done.

He wasn't real happy about it and gave me an elbow in the ribs, but that was too bad. He was the guy who'd brought up the subject by waving the sandwich under my nose.

I felt no guilt about it, none. What I felt was quite a bit worse than guilt. That stinking mackerel gave me the worst heartburn I'd experienced in my entire career.

I burped dead fish all afternoon.

Who would put such rot into a sandwich?

I should have known better than to eat anything made by a bachelor cowboy.

I hate mackerel.

CHAPTER NINE

Bummer: I Get Drafted to Guard the Stack Lot

We got back to headquarters around four o'clock that afternoon. By that time, I had gone through the worst of the Toxic Mackerel Syndrome and had managed to survive.

Do you think I got any sympathy from Slim? Oh no. Every time my stomach chugged, filling the cab with the smell of his awful sandwich, he had to make a big deal out of it.

He even had the gall to say—you won't believe this—he even had the nerve to say, "Well, it serves you right for stealin' food from your pal."

In the first place, I hadn't *stolen* anything. I had merely claimed my rightful share of the sandwich he'd waved in front of my nose. In the second place, what kind of pal gives his dog poisoned mackerel?

Oh well.

Remember the bull that had torn down the stack lot fence? Well, guess who was back in the stack lot when we returned to headquarters.

Mister Bull. It had probably taken him all of five seconds to rub down the fence, and we found him eating the southwest corner out of the haystack. This was bad news.

See, once a bull has developed a taste for free-choice alfalfa hay, he tends to want more of it, not less. Bulls are so big and powerful, they go pretty muchly where they want to go. It will take them a little longer to trash a good fence than a bad one, but bulls have nothing better to do, and they will rub and push on a fence until they have it on the ground.

It was getting along toward evening. Slim and I were tired from a long day's work, and neither of us had the time or energy to fix fence or play chase games with that greedy bull. We ran him out of the stack lot again, and once again Slim patched up the fence.

I watched and tried not to reveal my true thoughts. I mean, it was obvious, wasn't it? As soon as we left for the night, the bull would return, tear down the fence, and go back to eating a hole in the haystack.

So what was the point of patching the fence again? It was wasted effort. Until Slim came up with a radical new plan, such as loading the bull in a trailer and hauling him to the other side of the ranch, this was an exercise in fertility.

But no one asked my opinion. I was merely Head of Ranch Security, and we've already discussed that tender subject. I merely observed and kept silent and tried to remember that Slim never learned anything the easy way. His motto for ranch work was: "There's five wrong ways of doing every job, and a guy ought to try every one of 'em, every time."

Okay, maybe that wasn't really his motto, but it sure described what I had seen over the years. No, until he came up with some radical new . . .

HUH?

He had the rope tied into my collar before I knew what was happening. I mean, I was just sitting there, lost in deep thoughts about Improved Ranch Management, and I'd hardly noticed that he'd slipped down to the machine shed and returned with twelve feet of cotton rope. And before I had time to smell a rat and run for cover, he had tied one end of the rope to my collar.

No doubt my face showed shock and surprise.

I gazed up at him with hurt-filled eyes, whapped my tail on the ground, and asked, "What does this mean? You've tied a rope to my collar, and surely you're not planning ..."

He gave me a wink and a grin. "I've got it figgered, Hankie. It's time for some radical action."

What? Hey, if he thought he was going to stake me out and make bull bait out of me, he was badly ... I had plans, a schedule to keep, a ranch to run. I was a very busy dog and ...

No thanks. I pointed myself to the west, hit Full Flames on all engines, and ... GULK ... that dinky cotton rope proved to be stouter than you might have supposed, and I found myself lying on my back, looking up at my former friend.

"Hi, puppy. I've got a little job for you."

Ha! Forget that. Not me, brother.

"It'll be fun."

Oh sure, right. No thanks.

"Here's the deal. Me and you are going to make camp in the stack lot tonight."

Oh? Both of us? Well, maybe that wouldn't be ... I mean, if he was going to stay, it might be okay. Even fun.

"We're going to make camp, just me and you, 'cause we're such wonderful pals and camping buddies."

Yes, we'd had a pretty good relationship. A cowboy and his dog.

"And once we've made camp, I'm going home to my nice soft bed, and you're gonna be our official ranch representative when the bull comes back."

WHAT? I stared at him. I could hardly believe my ears.

Oh cruel world! Oh broken trust and wounded pride! What a fool I'd been. I should have eaten his whole sandwich when I'd had the chance. Instead of making a little stain on his pickup seat, I should have opened up the main valve and flooded the place.

Okay. Fine. It appeared that I had no choice in the matter. If he was enough of a rat to make bull bait out of his loyal friend, I would stiffen my back and hold my head high and do my duty for the ranch.

My conscience was clear in the matter. His conscience, on the other hand, would torment him all night, all day tomorrow, next week, next month, and for the rest of his life. One day in the distant future, fate would bring us back together. I would still be holding my head high, but he would be . . .

I didn't know what. He would be a begger, a tramp, a ragamuffin, a broken heap of a man who had tried to forget that awful night in March . . .

April . . . May . . . whenever it was that he had staked out his friend on a stake and left him to fight off the assault of a herd of bellowing bulls.

Okay, one bull, but he was a big bull.

What a cheap trick. I should have known he'd come up with some lousy job, but I'd been a fool, a trusting fool. I'll say no more about it.

Yes I will. I want this entered into the record. Notice that his solution to the bull problem didn't involve any posthole digging. That tells you all you need to know about Slim. With that, I shall rest my case.

We marched over to the patched fence. I marched with my head high and a look of steely resolve in my eyes, a proud member of the elite Ranch Security Forces. He, on the other hand, slumped along because he was already struggling under the terrible weight of his guilty conscience.

Life would be hard for him after this. I almost felt sorry for him.

No I didn't. I felt sorry for ME! Surely he wouldn't actually go through with this. Surely he'd change his mind and . . .

He tied the other end of the rope to a corner post. He bent down and patted me on the head— as though that was some big deal and would make up for sticking me on a lousy guard job.

"Well, here's our camp. Pretty nice place, huh?"

I glared daggers at him.

"And I want you to know, Hankie, that I sure appreciate you volunteering for this job."

Ha. What a joke.

"And it just breaks my heart that you get to camp out tonight, and I have to go home to a nice soft bed!"

Right. With dirty sheets.

He rubbed his chin and looked off to the west. "The way I figger it, he'll come back in the night for some more of that hay. All you have to do is give him a bark or two. I'm bettin' he'll take off running and won't come back."

Sure, and if he did happen to come back?

"But if he, does, just . . . you know, beat him up. Bite off his ears. You're the cowdog around here, and I'll bet you'll think of something."

I was thinking a LOT of somethings, and some of them involved Slim.

"Well, pleasant dreams, pooch. I'll check you in the morning. And I sure hope there ain't a bull in here. I'd be real disappointed."

And with that veiled threat, he left and walked back to the pickup. Well, he had sure done me dirt on this harebrained scheme, but there was one bright cloud on the silver lining. As he walked away, I was proud to note that he had a water stain on the seat of his britches. Tee hee. And he was scratching his behind. Served him right.

I listened to the whine of his pickup motor fade into the distance. A deep silence moved in around me, and also darkness. The sun was going down, don't you see, and when the sun goes down, it gets . . . well, dark, of course.

Burp.

And if I ever wanted to poison an enemy, I would feed him one of Slim's mackerel sandwiches.

Well, I did a scan of the horizon and saw no bulls. So far, so good. Maybe he wouldn't come tonight. Maybe he had gotten bored with tearing down fences and would go do something constructive. A guy could always hope.

But in the meantime, I needed to grab some sleep and revive my precious bodily fluids. Would I be able to sleep in this lonely outpost, knowing that somewhere out in the honk snork murging darkness there lurked a sassafras porkchop zzzz zzzzzzzzzzzz.

In other words, yes, I was able to sleep. In Security Work, we are forced to grab sleep when it's up for grabs, which often comes in short naps. I did manage to grab a short nap, but suddenly . . .

My ears flew up. I raised my head to an upright

position and checked Data Control. A warning light was blinking on the Earatory Scanners circuit. I hit three switches and threw all circuits over to Manual.

We were picking up strange unidentified noises. It appeared that my long night had just begun.

CHAPTER TEN

Surrounded by a Bunch of Urchin Cats

Pretty spooky, huh? Me all alone and tied up in the stack lot and hearing strange, unidentified sounds in the growing darkness? You bet it was, but what made it even spookier was that those strange sounds were not made by a bull.

I had no idea what they were. Shall I try to describe them? Okay, they weren't the deep bellowing of a bull but rather . . . well, high-pitched squeaks. If a guy tried to attach a word to the sound, he might describe it as "*mew*."

Hmmm. Very strange. I couldn't imagine what the source might be, although I was pretty sure that the mews were coming from something. But what? Big mice? Rats? Some new variety of night bird that I hadn't observed or cataloged or put into our database of night birds?

It was a puzzle. I homed in on the sounds and twisted my head to get better reception on the Earatory Scanner Network, but still . . .

I froze. Something was crawling through the weeds between me and the haystack!

How did I know? Simple. I could hear the swish and crackle of something moving, and I could also see the tops of the weeds quivering. A lot of dogs would have missed that last clue, the quivering weed tops, but I caught it. And all at once it occurred to me that the Whatever that was slithering through the weeds might be . . . a snake. Or even worse, several snakes.

Have we discussed my position on snakes? I don't like 'em, not even a little bit. I know what you're thinking: "Most snakes in the Texas Panhandle are harmless, including your bullsnakes, your coachwhips, your hognoses, your racers, and your gardening snakes. Only the rattlesnake is dangerous."

Ha! Don't tell me about bullsnakes being harmless. Try to play with one sometime and see what happens. I tried it once, and you know what he did? He coiled up, hissed, and struck me on the nose.

They are the most ill-tempered, unfriendly snakes on the ranch, and the fact that you won't die from their bite doesn't make getting bitten any fun.

No sir, I've got no use for a snake of any kind, and by George if those were snakes out there, slithering through the grass and weeds and coming in my direction, I was fixing to . . .

"Mew, mew."

Wait a minute, hold everything, halt. You thought those were snakes? Ha, ha. Not at all, and do you know why? You forgot a very crucial piece of evidence: snakes might hiss, but they don't mew. And here comes the real shocker. Do you know what kind of animal, vegetable, or mineral says mew?

You'll be shocked, stunned, surprised, and even embarrassed that you missed this piece of the puzzle, because it just happened to fit with some information we had already gathered in this case. Are you ready? Hang on.

Kittens. Baby kittens. Young cats.

No snakes at all. None. What a relief, huh? See, what you forgot was that, earlier in the day, we had uncovered and exposed a stray cat amongst the hay bales, and this same stray cat had *kittens*. Are you getting it now? I know, it's a little tough keeping track of all the clues and evidence that come flying at us from all directions, but . . .

Where were we? Oh yes, kittens. The weeds were alive with mewing kittens, and as we tracked their every movement through Data Control, we began to see a pattern emerging. They appeared to be heading, toward . . . ME.

Great. There I was on Night Guard, trying to protect our ranch's supply of winter fottage . . . forage, fodder . . . I was so-forthing the so-forth, and I was about to be joined by a herd of squeaking cats.

I needed that, and also three ringworms and a toothache. And another, bupp, mackerel sandwich, excuse me. Or to put it another way, the last thing I needed was a bunch of homeless vagabond yowling kittens.

I watered and witched. I waited and watched, shall we say, as the trails of quivering weed tops continued to move in my direction, and as the sounds of their mewing came closer. My ears were perked and fully alert, my eyes darted from weed to weed, and I noticed that my lip on the left side of my . . . well, mouth, of course, where else would you find a lip? . . . was beginning to rise into a snarl.

When the urchins popped out of the weeds, I would be ready for them.

They popped out of the weeds. Two of them. Three. Four? They kept popping out of the . . . five?

SIX? Good grief, this was turning into a convention of unwanted urchin cats!

They stared up at me. I glared back. They mewed. I snarled back. They were trying to look cute, you know, with their big smokey eyes and their little kitty faces and all that other stuff that cats use to weasel their way into the lives of others, but I wasn't fooled, not for a minute. I had been to school on cats, and I knew all their tricks, backward and forward.

Anyways, they mewed and tried to melt my heart with their so-called cuteness, and it didn't work. I stuck my nose right into the middle of them.

"Go home. Get a job. Chase a mouse. I don't like you."

Do you think they took a hint? Of course not. Cats don't take hints. Tell 'em, "Go away, I don't like you," and they think that means, "Oh goodie, a bunch of kitties, and will you please start rubbing on my legs and sticking your spiky little claws into my feet?"

That's just what they did. They were like . . . I don't know what. Ants. Flies. They gave me the creeps. It was time to go to sterner measures. I barked.

"Listen, you little brats. Go away and leave me alone. This is a Security Zone, and I have a job to

do. If I want company I'll call you, but don't hold your breath. Now scram. Scat."

They mewed and gave me pitiful looks and kept up their cuteness routine. Okay, I had given them fair warning. It was time to roll out my song about cats. Have we done it before? Maybe not. Here's how it went.

Cats from Little Kitties Grow

Now gather around, you kitties and kids. It's
    time for your cat education.
I'll tell you truth, the unvarnished truth,
    without tact or mere speculation.

There's a principal here, I want you to know.
    I assume that your momma forgot
To tell you the story of kitties and dogs, so
    I'll tell you it, like it or not.

The fact that you're here, the fact that you're
    mewing, the fact you've invaded my space
All tell me that you just don't get it at all
    and you're not comprehending your place.
So let me be blunt, go straight to the point.
    Little darlin's, you've got it all wrong.
You're cats. I'm a dog. Do you know what that
    means? It means that you'd better move on.

It's dangerous here, I want you to know. I'm
    not what you want me to be:
A kindly old grandpa, an uncle or friend,
    who'll take you upon his knee.
I'm mean and I'm gripy, too set in my ways
    to be nice to a gaggle of brats.
But the bottomest line I can tell you, my
    dears . . . is I don't like cats!

I know that you're cute little bundles of fur.
    You've only just started to grow.
But give you six months of mooching my
    scraps, and your true cattination will show.

You'll be fatter than Pete and twice as obnox-
   ious, and then you'll be driving me bats.
So kindly shove off, go away and get lost,
   'cause little kitties will grow into cats.

Pretty fine song, huh? You bet it was—maybe
not my very best, but you seldom get the very best
from a subject as dreary as cats. But it certainly
captured my feelings, and even more important . . .

It worked. Yes, it worked! After listening to my
song, all six kitties broke into tears and ran back to
wherever they had come from. To their mommy, to
their house of hay.

You probably think I felt like a louse, reducing
six kittens to tears. Not at all. Part of my job around
here involves being firm with cats. You have to keep
them humble, or they'll try to run the place.

If you want to have a nice garden, you have to
pull the weeds. That's my last word on the . . .

Okay, maybe chasing Pete was more fun than
making kittens sob and weep, but I didn't feel bad
about it. And just to be sure I wasn't tempted to feel
bad about it, I pushed it out of my mind. Totally and
forever. I turned my attention to the peace and
crying of the . . . that is, the peace and *quiet* of the
evening. Yes, it was a beautiful evening, so peaceful
and cryit . . . quiet, except for all the wailing and

moaning that was coming from the haystack.

What was the big deal? Why all the noise? Good grief, all I'd done was to sing them a little song and tell them the truth about Life. If they couldn't handle the truth, they were just a bunch of little crybabies. I had more important things to do than to worry about . . . phooey.

They weren't my problem, and don't forget that they were *stray cats* who had moved into our haystack without being invited, and they were trespassing. You know where I stand on the issue of . . .

Uh-oh. Here came Momma. No doubt she would throw a walleyed fit and accuse me of terrible crimes and maybe try to claw my face off. Well, she could try, but I had a few tricks for cats like her.

She didn't appear very threatening when she walked up to me. I mean, she wasn't humped up or hissing. Her ears weren't lying flat on her head, and her eyes didn't have that wild, crazy look cats get when they're about to turn on their buzzsaw of claws. Hmmm. Maybe it was a trick. I mean, she actually looked humble, if you can believe that. I wasn't sure I believed it.

Don't forget: never trust a cat.

She stopped several feet in front of me. She raised her chin and spoke in a . . . well, sort of a trembling voice. "Sir, my children said you told them to leave."

"Yes ma'am, that's the long and short of it."

"Were they bothering you?"

"Yes ma'am, I must admit that they were."

"They said you don't like cats."

"That's correct. Nothing personal, and don't get your feelings hurt. We just happen to be on opposite sides of the law, that's all."

She dropped her head. "I'm sorry the children bothered you. I know you're an important dog with many things on your mind. But you see, sir . . ." Her lip trembled, and she turned away. "They're hungry. They're still too young to hunt, and I'm not giving enough milk."

"I see. This may be too obvious to mention, ma'am, but I'm not a dairy dog. I don't give milk. Maybe you should be eating better. Then you could give more milk. I mean, you look kind of skinny to me." She started bawling. "Okay, you look thin, svelte . . . uh . . . lean . . . gaunt . . . pleasantly gaunt, so to speak."

"No" she cried, "you had it right the first time. I've become a skinny old hag. But there's never time for me to hunt food. I give everything to my children, and at the end of the day, I'm out of milk and so tired, all I can do is crawl into bed."

"Hmm, yes, I see. So you've come over here to ask for a handout, right? Free food and maybe a place in the machine shed, right?"

She stopped crying and stared at me. "No sir, that's not why I came over here. I came to apologize because my children were bothering you. I'm trying to teach them manners. I'm trying to teach them right from wrong. It's not right that they were disturbing you, and it won't happen again. Good evening, sir."

She turned and walked away. Well, it appeared that I had just scored another moral victory over the cats.

CHAPTER ELEVEN

The Bull Comes
and Attacks the
Poor Cats

But somehow I didn't feel too proud of myself. "Wait a minute. Don't get your tail in a wringer. I wasn't trying to insult you."

She stopped. "Yes sir, but you did."

"Okay, I'm . . . let's say that I was misquoted."

"Does that mean you're sorry?"

"No, it means . . . look, lady, let's don't get too picky. I'm Head of Ranch Security, and you're squatting on my ranch. Let's just say that I'm sorry I was misquoted."

Her voice was soft but firm. "We may be squatters in your haystack, but we have our pride, and we ask for nothing. As soon as the children can travel, we'll be leaving. You weren't misquoted, and you're not sorry you insulted us. Good evening, sir." She turned to leave again.

"Wait. Will you just hold your horses?" She stopped and looked back at me. I ground my teeth together and prepared to say the most painful words in the language. "Okay, I'm sorry."

Boy, that hurt, almost killed me.

"Thank you. It's nice of you to say so." Her gaze went to the rope. "Are you tied up?"

"Not exactly tied up, ma'am. I've been given a very important assignment. You see ..." And I told her all about the bull and so forth.

She nodded. "Yes, we've seen him. He's huge. I worry that he might harm the children. Do you think he might?"

I chuckled at that. "He might think about it, ma'am, but as long as I'm on duty, he won't come back into the stack lot. That's a guarantee. Your kids are safe. Oh, and by the way, if they want to wander over this way, it'll be all right. No problem."

"It's their bedtime, but thank you. May I call you Hank?"

"Sure, why not? And maybe you have a name too, huh?"

"Gertie. Good night, Hank. I wish you luck with the bull."

"Don't need luck, Gertie, just brute strength and a brilliant mind. But thanks, and say good night to the kids."

She went back to her place in the haystack. I watched until she disappeared in the gathering darkness. She definitely needed a few square meals. She was as skinny as a pencil, but not a bad old gal . . . for a cat, of course.

I had just turned toward the west and was watching the flashes of lightning in a storm cloud, when who or whom do you suppose came scampering up? Mister Stub Tail. The Original Cotton King. Drover.

"Hi Hank. I wondered where you were, and here you are, and I'll be derned, they've got you tied up. Are you guarding the kitties? Gosh, that's nice. They sure are cute."

I glared at the runt. "No, I am not guarding the kitties. I'm not nice, and I don't care that the kitties are cute. I'm guarding the haystack."

"Oh, how fun."

"Right, and maybe you'd like to help!"

"Sure, you bet. I love being a guard. Makes me feel important." He plopped down beside me and wrinkled his face into a . . . well, he probably thought it was a ferocious expression, and then he tried to growl. It was more of a squeak. "Oh yeah, this is fun. What are we guarding against?"

"The bull, Drover, the same bull that tore down the fence." The lights went out in his head, and his eyes turned into empty holes. "Hello? Are you there?"

All at once he was on his feet, dragging himself around in a circle. "Darn the luck! I don't know why this old leg picks the very worst times to go out on me. I was all set to help you and have some fun, but . . . oh my leg! It's killing me."

"Forget the leg, Drover, and get into Guard Formation. You can do this job on three legs."

He began backing away. "Well, I'd love to stay, Hank, I really would, honest, but I don't think I could stand the pain. It's getting worse by the second."

"Ignore it, Drover. We all must learn to live with pain."

He kept backing away. "Yeah, I'll try to live with it, but I think I'll live with it down at the gas tanks."

"Drover, halt! Come back here immediately, and that's a direct order."

"Yeah, but you're tied up, and I'd better rush this leg down to my old gunnysack. See you around, Hank, and good luck with the bull."

"Drover! Come back here, you little weenie! You'll

pay for this. I'm going to put this in my report."

"Take care of the kitties."

And with that, he vanished into the darkness. One of these days, Drover is going to pull that leg business once too often and get himself . . . oh well. I would be better off without him.

I tried to forget about Drover and turned my gaze back to the southwest. That line of thunderclouds seemed to be moving in our direction, twinkling with flashes of lightning and giving off an occasional grumble of thunder. Well, our grass could use a nice rain, but I could think of better places to be . . .

Suddenly I found myself staring into the eyes of a bull! I mean, he was right there in front of me, with his nose six inches away from my nose. His head was huge and ugly, and there was meanness in his eyes.

He spoke. "What are you doing here?"

"I . . . I'm not sure. That is, I was just . . . uh . . . watching the clouds . . . hoping for rain. I'm sure you'll agree that we could use a, well, rain. You know, the grass."

No change in his expression. "I'm fixing to take out this fence. You got any objections?"

"Take out the fence? You mean, tear it down?"

"Yeah."

"Well, to be real honest, my partners and I kind of wanted to leave it where it is. You see, it was put here to protect the, uh, stack lot, so to speak."

"Yeah. But I don't like fences."

I could feel his hot breath on my face. "It is an ugly fence, isn't it? I've said that many times, no kidding I have, but as far as tearing it out, I don't think . . ."

"I'm fixing to take it out. What about you?"

"Oh no, I'll just watch, thanks."

He brought his nose even closer to my face. I could smell him now. He smelled . . . huge. "What I'm asking, dumbbell, is do you want me to take *you* out with the fence, or would you like to move? 'Cause once I get started, I tend to ignore the screams of the wounded."

Gulp. "The screams of the wounded? Gee, you're serious about this, aren't you?"

"Yeah. I want that hay. Shall we fight about it?"

"Oh no, I've always felt that . . . what would you like for me to do, Mister . . . what was your name again?"

"Crash. They call me Crash Bull."

"Nice name."

"Shut up."

"Yes sir."

"Go over there and lie down. Don't get in my way.

108

Don't make a peep. Don't move a hair. Maybe I'll leave you a few bites of hay."

"Well . . . ha, ha . . . thanks a bunch, but dogs don't actually . . ."

"Shut up. I'm coming through."

"Right-o."

I got out of the way just in time, sprinted out to the end of my rope, and laid myself flat out on the ground. Crash was well named. You wouldn't believe what an easy job he made of taking out that fence. I mean, he didn't run at it or show much effort at all. He just leaned against it and then walked through it.

Over the snap of broken posts and wire, I heard him say, "Piece of cake, piece of cake."

I watched all of this by rolling my eyes. I mean, he had forbidden me from making peeps and moving hairs, but he hadn't said anything about rolling my eyes. So I laid there like a log . . . and tried not to think about what Slim would say in the morning. Oh brother. I had a feeling that he wouldn't understand.

Crash flattened the fence and then gave it the further insult of walking across it. That barbed wire had no more effect on his thick hide than the bite of a flea. With the muscles rippling across his massive shoulders, he lumbered over to the stack and . . . uh-oh, headed straight toward the bale where Gertie Cat and her family had made their home.

"Uh . . . Mister Bull? Crash? Excuse me, but I'd like to point out . . ."

His head shot around. "Shut your trap, or I'll stomp you all the way to China."

Well . . . I had tried. Too bad for Gertie Cat. Her home was about to be destroyed, eaten by a monster bull. I could only hope that she would be able to save the family. Gee whiz, if that bull stepped on one of those . . .

But you know what? Life sometimes plays amazing tricks and provides us with very strange twists. Crash probably weighed two thousand pounds. He was so strong and heavily armored that he could walk through barbed wire. Gertie cat weighed . . . what? Two pounds, three pounds with a full load of milk? A scrawny little cat, in other words, who couldn't have knocked a hole in a wet paper sack.

But she had a secret weapon, something no bull in history had ever possessed. *She was a mother.* That turned out to be a force more powerful than bone and muscle, barbed wire and cedar posts . . . and even fear.

Here's what happened. I witnessed it with my own eyes. Crash Bull lumbered over to the bale of hay, took hold of it with his huge jaws, picked it up, and gave it a shake. Suddenly and out of nowhere, that skinny mother cat came flying out of the darkness, jumped into the middle of Crash's face, and began buzzsawing him with all four feet and a mouthful of spikes.

And you talk about noise! You never heard such squalling, screaming, screeching, shrieking, hissing, yowling, and growling! That old gal sounded worse than thirty-seven nightmares full of vampires and monsters.

Crash Bull was stunned. He didn't know what had taken hold of him. He grunted so loud that I could feel the shock waves of it. He charged away from the haystack, sending bales flying in all directions and throwing up a cloud of dust and alfalfa leaves. Then he pointed himself to the south, took out that whole side of the fence, and ran for his life—wearing Gertie Cat all over his face, and her still tearing him up with her buzzsaws.

All I could say was . . . WOW! That was the bravest, toughest skinny little mother cat I'd ever met, and fellers, she won my respect right there. By the time she got back, I'd already chewed my rope in half and was making plans to move her family into a new home.

Motherhood
Wins the Day!

I know, she was just a cat, and I don't like cats, but there comes a time when a guy is forced to deal with Life as It Actually Happens. Gertie Cat had won my heart. A storm was coming, the bull had destroyed her shack of hay, and by George, we were fixing to move her into the machine shed.

I picked up one of the kittens in my enormous jaws—very carefully, by the way, which wasn't my usual style, but I'd seen Gertie do it—I picked up the kitten and was heading out of the stack lot when Gertie came walking back.

We met. I tried to speak, but I had a mouthful of . . . well, kitten, so my greeting was a bit garbled. Well, she stopped, sized me up with one quick sweep of her eyes, and addressed me in a quiet tone of voice.

113

"Put down my child."

WHAT? I just stood there, too shocked to move or speak or do anything. She went on.

"I know you don't like us and you want us to leave. I know you're big enough to whip me and make it look easy, but Buster, your face'll look like fresh liver."

I let the kitten slide out of my mouth. "Hey Gertie, there's a storm coming. Let's get these kids down to the machine shed before it hits."

She stared at me. "Are you serious? I thought you hated cats."

"Ma'am, could we save the heavy philosophical questions for later? I don't know what I think of cats, to be honest about it, but I know that you're one heck of mother and you need a warm, dry place for these kids."

She started . . . I couldn't believe it . . . she started crying. "I'm sorry. I lost my head. I try to be polite to everyone. I hate for my kids to see me this way, but sometimes I just . . . oh, I'm a terrible mother!"

"No ma'am, you're a wonderful mother. You saw what needed to be done, and you did it. You didn't think about it or argue about it. You just went out and . . ." I had to laugh. "By George, gal, you did thrash that bull."

She smiled through her tears. "Yes, I guess I

114

did, but if he came back again, I'd probably faint. I was so scared, I didn't know what else to do."

"Heh. You did right, and you did well." A rush of damp wind blew over us. "Let's get these kids moved. Grab a cat, and let's go."

I picked up my kitten and made a dash for the machine shed. The wind was swirling, and the air was filled with dust when I rounded the southeast corner. There I ran into . . . guess who. Drover.

He stared at me and stared at the kitten in my mouth. He let out a gasp. "Oh my gosh, Hank, what are you doing?"

"Arp muff ruff ork fuff muff."

"I can't understand you. I think you've got a cat in your mouth."

I set the kitten down and faced the runt. "I'm transporting a kitten, Drover. Do you mind?"

"Well, I was afraid you were going to . . . but you wouldn't do that, would you?"

"It's fixing to rain. We're moving the kittens inside."

"Aw heck. You're helping them? Gosh, how sweet. You're helping a poor mother cat and her little babies. That's about the sweetest thing I ever heard, and I think I'll just cry."

"Fine. You stand out in the rain and cry. Or

maybe you could lend a hand. Go grab a kitten and help us."

"Well, you know this old leg of mine . . . and I'll bet they don't taste very good, and they might have fleas."

Sometimes . . . oh well. He was worthless. He was born worthless.

I picked tip my kitten, left Drover to sniffle, and rushed into the machine shed. I dropped Kitty Number One and went back for another. Gertie and I passed each other coming and going. We each made three trips, and at last we got the job done. By then, the wind was rattling the tin on the machine shed, and the rain was making a roar on the roof.

We found a little pile of gunnysacks near the back of the shed. I fluffed them up with my front paws, and that's where we parked the family. Gertie and I gave each other a smile, and we sat down to rest and enjoy the sounds of the storm.

"Well, Gertie, it's a little dusty in here, and the gunnysacks don't smell too great, but it's not a bad place to be on a stormy night."

"Yes. Thank you, Hank. I know this must have been hard for you, helping a family of cats, but we appreciate it, don't we children?" They all clapped and cheered.

It kind of embarrassed me, to tell you the truth,

so I changed the subject. "Hey, we've got a good supply of Co-op dog food in that bowl over there. You and the kids help yourselves. We need to get a little meat on your bones. I mean, any mom who goes around fighting bulls needs to stay in shape."

She got a laugh out of that, but then I noticed that her expression grew dark. She seemed to be staring at something near the door.

She spoke in a low whisper. "Hank, who is that over there?"

"Oh, it's probably just Drover. He's my . . ."

It wasn't Drover. It was Pete, staring at us with those weird yellow eyes and twitching the last two inches of his tail. Oh, and you know what else? He had turned on his police-siren yowl, and there he sat, staring and yowling.

The next thing I knew, Gertie had flattened her ears, raised a strip of hair down her back, and turned on her own police-siren yowl. I darted my eyes from one cat to the other. This wasn't making much sense.

"Hey Gertie, I don't know what you're seeing over there, but what I'm looking at is just a cat."

"I know, and I don't like him. Who is he?"

"That's Pete, our local barncat. He's fat and spoiled and lazy and generally a sourpuss but probably harmless."

"He doesn't want us to stay."

"Hmmm. What makes you think so? I mean, you two haven't even met."

She broke her concentration long enough to look up at me. "Cats don't have to meet or talk. We're subtle, you know. The angle of an ear, the way we walk, a gaze that lingers—they all say something."

"I'll be derned. So what is Pete saying?"

Her eyes went back to Pete. "He's jealous. He doesn't want any competition. He thinks this is his ranch, and he wants to keep it that way."

Well, *that* got my attention. "Oh really? How foolish of him to have such wild thoughts. Maybe I should have a little talk with him. Would that make you feel better?"

"Much better. I don't trust him around the children."

"Let not your heart be troubled. I'll be right back."

I lumbered over to Pete. He watched me with hooded eyes and an odd smirk on his mouth. "Evening, Pete. Nice rain, huh?"

"Who are they, Hankie, and why are they here?"

"They're friends of mine, Gertie Cat and her six kittens."

His smile soured. "How nice. Six whining brats to disrupt our peace and quiet. They'll be leaving soon, I hope."

"They'll stay as long as they want. They're my special guests. Is there any particular reason why you're here, yowling and glaring at them? You're making Gertie feel unwanted."

His eyes popped open and he flashed a gleeful smile. "Really! She's very observant, and after she observes me for a couple of hours, I think she'll be ready to leave."

I chuckled. "Won't happen, Pete. Sorry."

"It'll happen, Hankie. You just wait and see." He swung his eyes back to Gertie and turned up the volume on his growl. She gathered her kittens around her and cast worried glances in our direction. "See? She's already thinking of moving out. Some cats, such as me, have amazing powers over others."

"No kidding!"

"It's true, Hankie." Suddenly his eyes were locked on me, and he was flicking the end of his tail back and forth in the air. "And what works on cats can work on dogs too. Just watch the end of my tail, Hankie. Back and forth, to and fro, watch the tail, nice and slow."

"Hmm. I'm feeling sleepy all of a sudden."

"Um-hm, you're feeling sleepy, and on the count of three, you will drift off into a nice, deep sleep, and you won't wake up until tomorrow morning. And you'll never be any the wiser."

"Mercy. I can't seem to . . . snork morf . . . keep my eyes . . ."

"Just let them drift shut, Hankie, as you float away on a big, soft feather bed."

"Feathery clouds drifting snorkly amork."

"One. Two. Three. You're asleep now. You're out of here, Hankie. You're history."

How could I have fallen asleep? How could I have let down my friend Gertie? How could I have been so dumb as to fall for Pete's sneaky trick of hypnopotomizing me with his tail?

Heh, heh. Watch this.

My eyes popped open. "Nope, didn't work, Pete, sorry. And now you're out of here." I snatched him up in my jaws, and let me tell you, fellers, that was one surprised cat. Heh. Trying to pull that watch-the-tail business on the Head of Ranch Security! What a dumbbell.

I hauled him to the door, drew back my head, and slung him out into the pouring rain. He landed in a big mud puddle. When his head came up, he looked like a drowned possum.

"Stay out of the machine shed and leave my

friends alone, you selfish, ill-tempered little scorpion. And I hope you enjoy the moisture."

Well, what a perfect ending to the day, throwing my archenemy (who hates water, by the way) into a mud puddle. I loved it.

Holding my head at a triumphant angle, I marched back to Gertie and the kids and received a hero's welcome. Pretty nice ending to the story, huh? Gertie had helped me keep the bull out of the stack lot, and I had provided her family with a home.

Yes, I know it was a little confusing. I, a dog who didn't like cats, had come to the rescue of a cat and six kittens, and in the process had given the bum's rush to a cat who didn't like cats, while Drover, who did like cats . . .

Oh well. All I do is tell them stories. It's not my job to explain them.

Case closed.

No, wait a second. There's one last matter, and you may find this hard to believe. The next morning, Slim *rebuilt* that whole south fence around the stack lot, and we're talking about new posts and handcrafted postholes, new wire that he actually stretched with wire stretchers, new staples, and a new braced corner.

Pretty amazing, huh? I know why he did it.

First, when the bull ran away with Gertie wrapped around his face, he vaporized the whole south fence. In other words, even Slim couldn't patch it. And second, the rain softened the ground so much that even a lazy hired hand could dig postholes in it. Slim would never admit that, but we dogs know the truth.

Just thought you might be interested.

See you around.

Case closed.

Have you read all
of Hank's adventures?

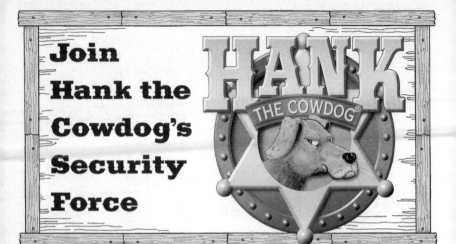

Join Hank the Cowdog's Security Force

Are you a big Hank the Cowdog fan? Then you'll want to join Hank's Security Force. Here is some of the neat stuff you will receive:

Welcome Package
- A Hank paperback of your choice
- Free Hank bookmarks

Eight issues of *The Hank Times* with
- Stories about Hank and his friends
- Lots of great games and puzzles
- Special previews of future books
- Fun contests

More Security Force Benefits
- Special discounts on Hank books and audiotapes
- An original Hank poster (19" x 25") absolutely free
- Unlimited access to Hank's Security Force website at www.hankthecowdog.com

Total value of the Welcome Package and *The Hank Times* is $23.95. However, your two-year membership is **only $8.95** plus $3.00 for shipping and handling.

□ Yes, I want to join Hank's Security Force. Enclosed is $11.95 ($8.95 + $3.00 for shipping and handling) for my **two-year membership**. [Make check payable to Maverick Books.]

Which book would you like to receive in your Welcome Package? Choose any book in the series.

(#   )   (#   )

FIRST CHOICE   SECOND CHOICE

                                             BOY or GIRL

YOUR NAME   (CIRCLE ONE)

MAILING ADDRESS

CITY   STATE   ZIP

TELEPHONE   BIRTH DATE

E-MAIL

Are you a □ Teacher or □ Librarian?

Send check or money order for $11.95 to:

Hank's Security Force
Maverick Books
P.O. Box 549
Perryton, Texas 79070

DO NOT SEND CASH. NO CREDIT CARDS ACCEPTED.
Allow 4–6 weeks for delivery.

The Hank the Cowdog Security Force, the Welcome Package, and The Hank Times *are the sole responsibility of Maverick Books. They are not organized, sponsored, or endorsed by Penguin Putnam Inc., Puffin Books, Viking Children's Books, or their subsidiaries or affiliates.*